PROMISE FOREVER

HARLAND CREEK SWEET ROMANCE

JODI ALLEN BRICE

CHAPTER 1

Gabriela Jackson shoved down the butterflies in her stomach and held her head up high as she walked down the sidewalk of Main Street. Armed with the only weapons she possessed. A haughty expression and her sharp tongue, she was ready for any verbal attacks.

For most people coming back home was like a balm to the soul.

But for Gabriela it was like throwing gasoline on a gaping wound.

She stopped at Bettie's Boutique when a pair of bright red heels caught her eye.

Stacey Landers, the owner, spotted her through the window and rushed to the front door.

She opened the door and poked her head out. "You're not welcome to shop in my boutique. And you can't loiter on the sidewalk. It's a crime." Her lips curled into a cruel smile.

Gabriela's blood froze in her veins. The past never truly stayed dead.

Composing herself, Gabriela smirked, "Believe me Stacey, this is the last place I'd be caught dead." She flipped her hair over her shoulder and sauntered away like she didn't have a care into world.

Truth be told, she had cares, more than anyone could know and they were weighing her down like a fully loaded gravel truck traveling over the potholes of her soul.

She spotted the Roses and Lace Flower Shop and debated ducking in there for a while. While they were not best friends, Olivia McCade had always been kind to her.

But she had a job to do. The sooner she completed it the sooner she could get out of town and back to her Aunt Agnes's farm.

She resisted the urge to hide in the Roses and Lace Flower Shop and steeled her resolve to her destination ahead.

The English Rose Bookstore.

All the ladies of Harland Creek, both young and old, spoke with unabashed adoration about Colin Bennett. Not only was he the owner of the bookstore, but he was supposedly a writer. But Gabriela knew it wasn't his occupation that made the women of Harland Creek speculate about Colin. It was his accent.

His British accent.

Not much was known about him except that he'd bought the old bookstore when Mrs. Willis sold it to move into the nursing home. It was reported that he was charming and kind to everyone that walked into his establishment.

When it came to men, Gabriela knew that underneath a deceptive charming veneer, lay a more sinister side.

Gabriela gripped the old ugly green and orange tapestry bag which held tiny jars of honey tighter to her body.

She didn't understand why her Aunt couldn't invest in something newer, something more attractive than the worn out carpetbag she'd had for ages.

She groaned inwardly when she spotted the bookstore a

few feet away. She wished her aunt would have made the delivery instead of insisting Gabriela lend a hand. Agnes Jackson was as stubborn as a mule and mean as a snake.

Her parents had up and ran off to Boca Raton and left her no living relative in Harland Creek except her old aunt. Now she was stuck at staying at Aunt Agnes's for the time being. And for the time being , she had to coddle the old woman.

She glanced at the sign on the book store window. "Quilter's retreat every Thursday at nine a.m. Everyone welcome."

"Right. Everyone except me." Gabriela spit out under her breath.

She reached out her hand and steeled her spine. The bell over the door dinged as she stepped inside.

Missy Long's eyes widened when she saw Gabriela. Sensing there was competition near her prey, Missy leaned over the counter to the owner and batted her ridiculously long eyelashes. "Now Colin, tell me which book I should read first."

Gabriela glanced at the three books stacked on the counter. Each clearly marked book one, book two, book three.

She met the bored eyes of the Englishman and waited to hear what he would say.

"Ms. Long, I suggest this one," he picked up book one and gave her a polite smile.

"I can't thank you enough for recommending this author who is new to me. I'm sure I will enjoy her work."

"Actually that author is a man." Gabriela stated.

"You need glasses, Gabriela. The name is clearly Jessica McLaurin." Missy lifted her pretty chin in the air.

"Jessica McLaurin is a pen name. His real name is Mac Earls." Gabriela snorted.

"That's impossible. Men don't write romance." Missy looked at Colin for affirmation.

Something in his gaze shifted.

Gabriela rolled her eyes. "I'm dropping these off for Agnes Jackson. " Gabriela set the bag of honey jars on the counter.

"Right, Gabriela. I know your game. I've already warned Colin about you." Missy glared.

"Oh yeah. What did you say?" Gabriela gave her an amused smile.

"I told him the truth. That you're a man eater." Missy narrowed her eyes.

"Good thing I'm plum worn out otherwise, Mr. Fancy Pants might be in trouble." Gabriela did her best Southern drawl and stifled a yawn with the back of her hand.

Colin shot her an odd look. A look that read he'd heard the rumors about her, yet he was still oddly curious.

Missy spun around ready to engage in a verbal battle. Gabriela was ready for the woman and crossed her arms over her chest. Just then the bell over the door tinkled as the Pastor of the Baptist church entered.

"Hello Colin, hello ladies." Pastor John gave everyone a smile.

"Hello, Pastor John." Colin's deep voice filled the book-store. 'How are you today?"

"Fine, Colin, just fine." He smiled and nodded towards the back of the room. "I heard that the quilting group is in the back of your store?"

"Yes. They reserved the reading space every Thursday at nine a.m. While it seems to be working well when they are hand piecing their blocks I'm not so sure it will be big enough to set up a quilt frame to finish the quilt."

"Ah, I see." A strained look crossed the pastor's face.

"They're already set up if you want to go back there." Colin offered.

Pastor John held up his hands and shook his head. "No thank you. I've really got to be going."

"Pastor, do you still need more volunteers to help with the spaghetti supper? How many tickets have you sold?" Missy slapped on an angelic smile.

"Just about everyone has bought a ticket for a plate. But so far it's not as much as we expected to raise for Wilma's cancer treatment."

"Why don't you have a silent auction. You'd make more money." Gabriela lifted a hardback book off the shelf and gently turned the pages.

Pastor John turned his attention to her. "Silent auction?"

"Yeah. Just get everyone to donate something. People write down their bids and at the end of the night announce who has the highest bid. You'll be surprised how competitive people get when they think they have something someone else wants." She gave a look at Missy.

Missy glared.

"Yes, that's a great idea Gabriela." Pastor John smiled. "Everyone in Harland Creek has something to offer. Flowers from Olivia's shop, honey from your aunt, a quilt…"

"I'll donate a complete series of books signed by an author." Colin offered.

"Those are good things but you should also consider, auctioning someone off for a date." Gabriela snorted and ran her finger down the spine of the latest mystery novel perched on a table. She'd not read this one yet.

"Like sex trafficking?" Missy shrieked.

"No, you idiot." Gabriela glared. "Like a dinner date. Or picnic or whatever."

'Would you be interested in being the one auctioned?" Pastor John cocked his head.

"No. I would not. If you want to make it interesting, you should get someone that no one knows anything about.

Someone of mystery. Like him." She shoved her thumb at Colin.

His eyes widened in offense. "Me?'

Pastor John frowned and looked between Colin and her.

"Oh Colin what a wonderful idea. And just think you'll be doing it for charity." Missy batted her eyes.

"That's not a bad idea." Pastor John rubbed his chin.

"I don't think your congregation would look favorably on this. After all it's a church event." Colin argued.

"Actually it's not a church event. It's a community event and we moved the spaghetti supper over to the Community building to hold more people."

"I don't think anyone will bid on me. You should get someone famous. Like Gabriela." Colin narrowed his eyes.

"Hey, don't drag me into this. I'm done with the whole stand here and look pretty thing. Now I have to actually work for a living." She sighed dramatically.

"Colin would you at least please think about it." Pastor John begged. "It would mean the world to Wilma."

Gabriela grinned. Good old Pastor John knew how to use sympathy to his advantage, Too bad it didn't work on his old bat of a sister that no one liked.

"Fine. I'll think about it. But just remember I haven't agreed to anything." Colin lifted his chin.

"Perfect." Pastor John clasp his hands together in triumph. "I've got to be going. Dropping by the hospital to visit with the patients. Missy, would you mind walking to my car with me. I Have some questions about the song you picked out for the choir for Sunday Service."

"Of course." She gave an angelic smile and picked up her books. She batted her eyes at Colin before shooting arrows and glares at Gabriela as she walked out the door.

"You shouldn't have volunteered me like that." Colin walked around the counter and stood in front of her.

He was taller than she realized. At five seven she was usually eye to eye with men. Not him. She had to actually look up to see his face.

She set down the book she'd been looking at and shrugged. "Easy, Downton Abby. Don't get your knickers in twist. I thought I was doing you a favor."

"A favor?" He glared. "Auctioning me off like a side of beef is doing me a favor?"

"Well, yeah. It will help you get to know the townspeople, put you in a favorable light, and maybe find you a girlfriend." She shrugged and pulled out the jars from her bag and placed them on the counter.

"I don't need any of those things."

"Don't you want the townspeople to stop gossiping about you?"

"Gossiping about me? I think you mean they are gossiping about you." He glared.

She froze. The old familiar knot in her stomach tightened.

"Then let me be a lesson. Put yourself in a light that will win them over and adopt you as one of their own. Otherwise you'll be like me, living in a town that hates you." She turned on her heel and walked out the door.

CHAPTER 2

*C*olin watched Gabriela walk across the street and disappear behind the courthouse.

He'd been in Harland Creek long enough to sense the dislike of her from the townspeople. He wasn't so bold as to actually come out and ask what Gabriela Jackson had done to make the town turn against her. He'd seen the glares and the spiky comments whenever her name was brought up.

But he'd also seen something else. The jealousy in other women's eyes when men turned to stare at her. Or how the men seemed to want to look but wouldn't want anyone to know about it.

Like a dirty secret.

He shook his head. The townspeople were probably right. She probably was a man eater.

To him, she was the epitome of the villainess in a novel who, in the end, would get what she deserved.

She was exactly the kind of women he intended to stay away from.

Since his escape from England and the scandal he'd found himself in, he vowed never to let a woman ruin his life again.

"Colin, I can't thank you enough for letting us use your space in the back." Elizabeth Harland dug around in her large bag that she'd brought her sewing in. "And I have some cookies for you. As a thank you."

"How wonderful. Thank you so much" Colin smiled and took the gift presented in a zip lock bag. "I'll certainly enjoy these with a cup of English Tea."

'That's what I was thinking." She smiled and patted his hand.

"Was that Gabriela's mouth I heard in here?" Agnes scowled as she appeared from behind a book case.

"You know good and well it was, Agnes." Elizabeth rolled her eyes.

"She didn't break any of the honey jars did she?" She picked up a jar and carefully inspected it.

"No, I don't think so…" Colin looked at the jars.

"Why didn't you just bring them when you came? You made Gabriela make an unnecessary trip into town." Elizabeth.

"I couldn't carry my quilting and jars of honey. Besides, she needs to be doing something instead of staying out all night."

"Out all night? Where does she go?"

"I have no idea. Probably doing something immoral. All I know is she disappears at night and I hear her come in when I get up to make coffee at five. She sleeps all day and has no motivation. She had the world by the tail and threw it away because she has no drive."

"If I recall, you didn't have much motivation when you were young. You used to sleep all day." Elizabeth arched a brow.

"Only during the summer. You act like I was lazy." Agnes snarled.

"All I'm saying is you were young once. Don't be so judgmental." Elizabeth shrugged.

"I know that tigers don't change their strips." Agnes pointed her finger at Elizabeth.

Elizabeth sighed and looked at Colin. "Thanks again for letting us meet here."

Colin smiled. "Of course. I hope you found the atmosphere to your liking."

"Oh yes. There is something lovely about sewing in a room full of books."

"Shall I put you down for next Thursday?"

"Yes. We've decided to come here to sew our individual blocks and we'll go to the quilt shop to quilt since it's big enough for a quilt frame." Agnes nodded. She picked up a jar of honey and examined the label.

"I told her not to be putting that fancy label on it. I told her simple was best but Gabriela won't listen." She shook her head.

"I like it." Elizabeth looked at the label with elaborate script and a bee. "It looks refined. What do you think, Colin?"

"Very nice." He examined the jar. "Although what's inside is what matters."

"Exactly, right." Agnes nodded once. "Let's go. Donna is having us over for some soup and sandwiches. We'll see you later, Colin."

"Goodbye ladies." He watched the entire quilting group head out the front door after they had gathered their supplies.

They might squabble like a group of hens, but he saw the love and faithfulness there.

It was quite different than how he grew up.

His mind went back to England. His mother and father would probably be planning on hosting another elaborate dinner party at their mansion. His brother Charles would be there with his new wife Margaret surrounded by friends and music and flowing champagne.

A small twinge in his gut reminded him that maybe moving across the ocean wasn't such a good idea. He'd been here two months, hoping to get further along in his novel.

But something was missing.

Something he couldn't quite get right. He took a sip of tea.

The bell of the door had him looking up. "Can I help…"

Gabriela darted past him. "I saw the silver shoe gang leave."

'The silver…." He slammed his mouth shut and followed her down an aisle. She stopped in the classical section. "You mean the quilting group." He lifted the cup to his lips.

"Yeah, yeah. You don't have to stand there and watch me. Missy should be darting back in here. Think she spotted me coming in. She'll come in here to make sure I don't have you sprawled out across the counter having my way with you."

He choked on his tea..

She cut her eyes at him and arched a perfect brow. "You okay there, Downton Abby?"

He cleared his throat and wiped the tea off his tie. "My name is Colin."

The bell tingled.

She waved him away and opened a Jane Austen book, carefully turning the pages and quickly forgetting him.

He walked back to the front of the bookstore and frowned. "Can I help you?"

"Yeah I was wondering if Gabriela was in here. I thought I saw her come in." He looked over Colin's shoulder

Colin frowned as Gabriela peeked out from one of the bookcases, her eyes wide. She met his eyes and slowly shook her head.

"I'm sorry. She was in here earlier but left." He held out

his hand. "I'm Colin Bennet. The owner of The English Rose. I don't think I've seen you in Harland Creek."

"You're the English guy all the women are swooning over." He held out his hand. "I'm Travis Lincoln. My father is President of the bank."

"Ah, yes. Nice to meet you." Colin nodded at the tea kettle. "Would you care for a cup of tea?" His eyes skittered back to Gabriela who scowled at him for keeping him instead of hurrying him on his way.

"Ah no." Travis wrinkled up his nose. "I'm more of a coffee guy. Well nice to meet you."

"Travis, if I see Gabriela I'll tell her you're looking for her." Colin offered.

"No. Don't do that." He shook his head and darted out the door.

"You can come out now." Colin called out.

Gabriela's face was pale and her eyes angry.

"Who was that guy?"

"No one." She straightened and lifted her chin.

"Why would you be hiding from no one."

She spun around and glared. "I wasn't hiding. I was avoiding. There's a difference."

He opened his mouth, but she cut him off.

"You didn't offer me any tea." She hefted the bag on her shoulder.

"Would you like some tea?" He frowned, surprised at himself for forgetting his manners.

She chortled. "Downton Abby, if I had some of your tea, the whole town would be over here trying to save you from my evil clutches." She walked past him to the door. Peering out the glass and making sure the coast was clear, she opened the door.

"Be careful in this town. People are friendly until they decide they don't like you. Next thing you know you're walking around with a scarlet letter splattered across your chest."

Her heels made clicking sounds as she walked down the sideway.

Gabriela Jackson was beautiful for sure. But he knew that women like her, could destroy a man in a minute.

CHAPTER 3

"Gabriela Jackson, open up this door right now." Agnes screamed on the other side of the locked door.

Gabriela squinted at the sunlight spilling into the room. She'd forgotten to close the curtains before she crawled into bed in the wee hours of the morning and now the light was blinding.

She glanced at the wind up clock on the bedside table. Ten o'clock.

"Ugh. Give me a minute." She called out to her aunt.

"Now, Gabriela." Agnes hollered.

"Unless you want to see me in my birthday suit I suggest you give me a minute." She snarled.

Agnes went silent.

Gabriela grinned.

She took her time climbing out of bed and putting on her short silk robe. When she finally opened the door Agnes looked like she was about to explode.

"Good morning to you." Gabriela gave her a bored look.

"Morning? It's almost lunch." Agnes stormed into the

cramped room. "I told you yesterday you needed to be up and ready today. We have a meeting."

"Meeting? " Gabriela arched her brow. "This isn't some kind of funeral arrangement meeting is it? Isn't that something you should have planned a few years back?"

Agnes pressed her lips into a thin line. "Girl, watch your tone with me. You know what meeting I'm talking about. The meeting for planning the silent auction."

"How'd I get involved in this?" She held up her hands.

"You gave the pastor the brilliant idea. Now he wants your input as to how to proceed." She smirked.

"I don't think anyone wants to see me at this meeting. Besides, I've got things planned for today." She stifled a yawn.

"Sleeping all day isn't a productive day. Now get dressed and I'll meet you downstairs." Agnes headed for the door.

"I'm not a child anymore. You can't just order me around." Gabriela glared.

Agnes turned slowly. "If you don't get dressed and get downstairs, then you'll be finding yourself homeless for the remainder of your stay in Harland Creek."

Gabriela maintained her stoic expression despite the pit in her stomach.

Agnes grinned like a fool and left.

CHAPTER 4

"*T*hank you so much for coming. We are working very hard to help raise enough money for Wilma's cancer treatment and extended stay. In Harland Creek we are like family and I know everyone wants to help. " Pastor John clasped his hands together as he stood in front of the community center filled with all the business owners of Harland Creek.

"What's this about a silent auction? I'd like to hear more about that." Elizabeth spoke up.

"Yes, well the idea was from Gabriela Jackson." Pastor john nodded slowly.

A low murmur went around the room.

Colin felt a little bad for the girl. He knew what it was like not to fit in.

"And I've done some research on the idea. Basically everyone donates something and the night of the charity supper people have a chance to walk around the room and write down what they bid. People can outbid others until the auction is over. Then the paper bids are taken up and winners are announced. Is that right, Gabriela?" Pastor John waited for her to answer.

"Yes." She held her chin high and tried to act nonchalant but he noticed how tightly her hand clenched in a fist.

"And there was a mention of an auction date?" Pastor John cocked his head. "I'd like to take a vote. To make sure this is something we want to pursue. Make sure it's ethical."

Snickers went up around the room.

"What's an auction date?" Agnes stood up and narrowed her eyes. "This isn't no sex thing is it? Cause I don't vote for that."

"We all know you haven't done sex in a century." Farmer Joe Smith snickered.

Giggles went up around the room.

The pastor's face went red.

Gabriela looked like she wanted to be sick.

"Well first you need someone that everyone wants to win a date with. I mean, we have some good looking folks here in Harland Creek but this has to be done with some rules." Elizabeth stood.

"I agree, Ms. Elizabeth." Pastor John nodded. "Let's make a list, shall we?"

"Rule number one. No intercourse." Agnes stuck her finger in the air. "We aren't running a prostitution ring here"

Colin cringed at the old woman's boldness. A few snickers went up.

"Agnes," Elizabeth hissed.

"What? I've seen the news. Young people these days think nothing of giving themselves away like a common.."

"Thank you, Mrs. Jackson, for your input." Pastor John mopped his forehead with his handkerchief.

Colin cut his eyes at Gabriela. She was as pale as a sheet.

"Rule number two. The person being auctioned gets to pick the place to have the date. And I think it wouldn't hurt if the owners of the restaurants offered to pick up the tab." Donna Williams stood up.

Everyone nodded and agreed.

"I'll donate some flowers for a bouquet that Olivia can make. For the date." Elizabeth smiled.

"Thank you Elizabeth. That's very generous." Pastor John smiled.

Elizabeth sat up a bit straighter.

Colin grinned. He'd heard about how the quilting ladies had gotten kicked out of quilting at the church because they were gossiping about the Pastor's sister. It was obvious they were trying to get back into his good graces.

"If you want to keep it clean then stop making it all romantic." Farmer Joe Smith stated.

"What do you suggest? You want the winning couple to have dinner with your pigs?" Agnes snarked. "They could even milk a cow or two."

"What's wrong with that?" Farmer Smith glared. "Why that's how I met my Myrtle, God rest her soul. We meet at a 4H meeting in high school. She had the best looking pig I ever did see this side of the Mississippi River."

Gabriela laughed.

Everyone turned and looked at her.

"Gabriela, do you have something to include? This was your idea anyway."

She sobered and looked around the room. Her gaze landed on Colin.

"Why don't you have the date be for the day in addition to dinner."

"Go on." Pastor John crossed his arms.

"Well, its July in Mississippi so it's hot. Why not kayak down the river, have a picnic, and then go ziplining."

"Harland Creek has a zipline?" Farmer Smith squinted.

"Yeah, Grayson put one in that goes across Harland Creek between his house and Elizabeth's." Pastor John nodded.

"He did it for Heather." Elizabeth giggled. "You should see her and Petunia going across it."

"I'm not sure about kayaking, but I like the idea of a picnic and zipline. Those sound really great. And I think we should still add the dinner. That would be a nice ending to a date." Pastor John nodded.

"So now all we have to do is get someone to volunteer to be auctioned." Donna cocked her head. "Someone that everyone is dying to go out with."

Agnes cut her eyes at Gabriela who was effectively ignoring her aunt.

"I volunteer Colin Bennet." Gabriela smirked.

He froze. All eyes were on him.

"I don't think that's a good idea." He shook his head. "You should get someone that's famous. Like Gabriela." He glared at her.

She snorted and crossed her arms. "Silly little English man. The point of having an auction is to have someone that people are willing to bid on."

The room went silent.

"You are who the town wants, Colin." Agnes nodded.

Something in his gut sunk. He cut his eyes at Gabriela. For the first time since he laid eyes on Gabriela, she looked wounded.

"Please Colin. It's for a great cause." Everyone stood and gathered around him. He caught a glimpse of Gabriela as she slipped out the door.

He knew it was no use fighting. "If it's for charity. Why not."

CHAPTER 5

*C*olin eased into the oversized chair and set his cup of English tea on the table. After the day he had he'd wished he 'd gotten something stronger. Ringo, his border collie placed his head on his knee and gave him a sympathetic look.

He smiled and rubbed the dog between the ears.

He couldn't believe Gabriela had offered him up like a Christmas goose to be auctioned off. She didn't even know him and she'd thrown him under the bus.

He should have argued harder instead of agreeing to go along with the crowd.

When would he learn?

Gabriela would have been a better candidate. After all, she was the famous supermodel.

He took a sip of his tea and something caught his eye out the living room window.

He stood and walked over to the window for a closer look. A figure outlined in white walked toward the tree line.

He frowned. He bought this cottage out in the middle of nowhere because he valued his privacy. The three bedroom, two bath house was over fifty years old. It needed cosmetic improvements but it was a solid house.

He peered out the window. Whoever it was seemed to be in no hurry.

He'd never had trespassers before. He'd gotten a few deer and raccoons wandering into his yard at night, but no one dared come near his house due to the rumors the lake behind his house was haunted.

He didn't believe in such nonsense but the figure in white did give him pause.

"This is ridiculous." He put his cup of tea down and grabbed a flashlight. "Come on Ringo."

He hurried out the front door, determined to put a stop to whoever was lurching about on his land. Ringo was at his side.

The figure headed into the woods before he could reach it. Ringo stiffened as he caught sight of the figure.

"Ringo, easy boy. Don't go running off." He muttered to himself.

The light of the flashlight played against the ground and trees. He caught a glimpse of white at the edge of the bank overlooking the water that flowed below.

The moon was bright and he cut the flashlight. Whoever it was draped in white was standing at the edge of the bank with their arms outstretched.

He moved closer and inhaled deep when he realized who it was. Ringo barked.

"What are you doing ?"

Startled she turned, losing her footing.

He lunged for her and grabbed her by the arm. He pulled her close against his body to keep her from going over the edge.

He stared down into Gabriela's face.

"Let go of me." She scowled

"Are you crazy?"

"Not generally." She snarked and stepped out of his hold. "I don't like strange men grabbing me."

He couldn't see her eyes but he bet she was shooting daggers at him.

"And I don't like strange women on my property." He shot back.

"Ah look at you, Downtown Abby. Being all snarky." She picked up a bag off the ground. Ringo sniffed her leg and then gave her hand a lick.

"Eww." She wiped the dog slobber off her hand.

"What are you doing here?"

"Skinny dipping." She cocked her head.

"You're still wearing your clothes." He countered.

"You got here too early. I was about to take off my clothes." She headed for the woods.

He turned on the flashlight and followed her.

She glared at him over her shoulder "What are you doing out here anyway?"

"I bought the cottage and fifty acres of surrounding land." He shone the light in her face.

She grimaced and batted the flashlight away. "Turn off that light. What are you eighty years old? There's enough light from the moon without that flashlight."

"I'm twenty-eight." He narrowed his eyes.

She stopped and frowned. "Really? I thought you were older."

"How old are you? I'm guessing barely twenty-one. Which means you are hitting your retirement age for modeling." He smiled at himself for his smart comeback.

"I see you know your models. I am actually twenty-two this September. I moved back to Harland Creek to check myself into the nursing home." She deadpanned and kept walking.

He snorted, caught off guard by her-self depreciating remark.

She groaned as the moon dipped behind the clouds, plunging them into darkness. "Well, come on Downton Abby, where's your flashlight. Don't stop now."She called out. "Or as you say in Merry old England. Torch."

He turned on the flashlight and caught up to her. "I have a bone to pick with you."

"Ah, I don't think that is a British colloquialism. What you should say, is bloody woman. How could you stick your nose in my porridge and volunteer me as an auction date."

"I don't speak like that." He glared. "But yes, you had no right to volunteer me as a date. I don't know many people here. I didn't want to give anyone the idea I'm looking for a girlfriend."

"Oh, don't you worry, Sherlock. No one would mistake you for being romantic." She turned and patted him on the chest. "In all reality you really should be thanking me."

"Thanking you? Are you serious?"

"Quite. Now not only will this boost your popularity with the townspeople in general for being so generous. You will be the hero of the day, and probably draw in more business for your bookstore. I bet they'll even take out an ad in the Jackson paper to advertise it so it will draw in more people." She smiled brightly

"More people?" Suddenly he felt nauseated.

"You'll probably have at least thirty women bidding on you. It's a win win for everyone."

"I think you should volunteer to be a date." He glared.

"You need someone people will bid on. No one would bid on me." She shrugged.

"I've seen how the guys looks at you . You could bring in a lot of money."

She stopped and looked at him. A sadness washed over

her face. "I'm not volunteering. If I did the townspeople would hate me more than they already do." She blinked and suddenly the permanent confidence was back in her beautiful features. "Besides, you might find your forever after girl. Who knows?"

"I'm. not looking for a forever after." He scowled.

"Oh, I just figured all you romantic authors look for the perfect love." She folded her hands in her chin in an angelic pose.

"You know nothing about me."

"True. So let's keep it that way." She snarked and headed back to the road.

"Wait a minute. You can't just trespass and then not tell me what you were doing on my land."

"I already told you. I was going to skinny dip."

"And I don't believe you." He countered.

"Whatever. Go to bed, Downton Abby." She headed toward the road.

He watched her disappear down the road. He listened, waiting to hear a car engine start. But he heard nothing.

He jogged over to the road and shone the light.

She was walking home.

That was impossible. It was almost five miles from his house to Agnes's. She didn't even have a flashlight. How was she going to make it in the dark. Not to mention what if some stranger stopped.

His chivalric side beat out his grudge holding side. He jogged back to the house and grabbed his keys.

He slid into this car and let Ringo jump in before he started the engine. He drove out of his driveway onto the road. He quickly caught up with her.

He stuck his head out the window. "Get in and I'll drive you home."

"No thank you."

He scowled. "You can't possibly walk all the way back home. It's almost five miles."

"Wow, I'm impressed. You didn't even use kilometers. Way to acclimate to the states, Oliver Twist."

"Stop calling me those stupid names." He gritted out .

"Oh, you're not a fan of Charles Dickens? I'm surprised. Aren't you supposed to be writing the next best novel?"

"Yes, I mean no." He shook his head. "Yes, I am a fan of Charles Dickens. And no I'm not writing the world's next best novel." Just the world's second best novel. But no need for her to hear that.

"Ah, gotcha." She pointed a perfectly manicured nail at him. "I never said world's next best novel. Your confidence has given you away, Downton."

"For goodness sake, will you…"

"Can't stay and chat." She held up her hand. "I've got to be going. Can't just stand around here all night." She narrowed her eyes at him. "Never know when some pervert will stop and try to offer me a ride." She turned on her heel like she was walking a runway and continued walking down the road.

She held up her arm as she left.

He wasn't quite sure but instead of a goodbye wave, he could have sworn under the pale moon light she was giving him the bird.

CHAPTER 6

*G*abriela woke up at what Aunt Agnes would deem a decent hour. Eight o'clock.

She would have slept late if she hadn't been bothered by that stupid Brit who wouldn't leave her alone to her nightly activities.

Instead she was forced to come home.

She'd had a fitful sleep and dreamed of things of the past. She preferred sleeping during daylight hours. That way her demons couldn't haunt her during the light.

She put her robe on and padded into he kitchen. Her aunt might be a grump but she made a good cup of coffee.

"Well, well, well. Look who's up?" Agnes put her empty honey jars in the sink and turned on the water. "If you want coffee, I drank it all. You'll have to make yourself a new pot."

"I don't know how." She lied.

"Now's the time to learn." Agnes turned and faced her. "Fill up the water first."

Gabriela didn't argue. At least now she'd know how to make the coffee where it wasn't bitter.

After she filled the reservoir with water, she put in the coffee filter and looked at Agnes.

"Four big scoops." Agnes nodded at the coffee pot.

She obeyed and then cut her eyes at Agnes. "I know you do something different with the coffee. Are you sure it's enough coffee?"

Agnes raised her eyebrows. "Fine. It's five scoops. And add a pinch of salt. It takes the bitterness out."

Gabriela smirked and added another scoop and the salt. She turned on the coffeepot. While she waited, she grabbed a coffee cup out of the cabinet.

"Someone dropped by and asked about you." Agnes washed each honey jar and put it to dry on the drying mat.

"Oh yeah? Was it David Beckham?" She sat in the chair and grabbed the morning paper.

"Wrong Englishman. It was Colin Bennett."

She slowly folded the paper and tried to act casual. "Oh yeah?"

"He asked if you got home okay last night." Agnes dried her hands and stared at her.

Gabriela felt the familiar pit in her stomach.

"Gabriela Jackson. Do not be messing with that man. He's a good man. He doesn't need you coming in and messing things up."

"Believe me, I want nothing to do with Colin Bennett." Gabriela stiffened her spine.

"Gabriela, I'm not kidding. This is someone who's found a home here in Harland Creek."

"Goodie for him." She said without enthusiasm.

Agnes slammed her hand on the kitchen table, making Gabriela jump. "I'm serious. Leave Colin Bennet alone."

Gabriela narrowed her eyes. "Or what?"

"Or else you'll find yourself without any family or place to stay in Harland Creek." Agnes warned.

She slowly stood and poured herself a hot cup of coffee.

She folded the paper and stuck it under her arm. "If you'll excuse me, I've got to get ready." She gave a small curtsey and headed back to her room.

She slammed the door when she stepped inside. Anger mixed with hurt welled up inside her. She wanted nothing more than to be done with her past.

She took a sip and grimaced.

Agnes had lied. The coffee still held a bitter taste to it.

Just like the small town of Harland Creek.

CHAPTER 7

$\mathcal{C}$olin had arrived early at the English Rose Bookstore to try to get some words written before opening for the day. He liked writing while it was still dark out and inspiration hit in the quietness of the early morning.

He sipped on his tea and scowled at the words on the computer.

He sometimes wished for the earlier days when a writer could rip a paper from their typewriter and dramatically throw it in the trash can.

Try as he may, he could not bring himself to delete the words he had struggled with for days.

He liked his story, but there was something about his heroine that was too ...likeable. Irritatingly likeable.

"Ugh." His finger hovered over the delete button but he couldn't press it.

Instead he typed in a small note in red to remind himself to come back to the scene when he had flushed out her character better.

He leaned back in his chair and studied the screen

After staring at the screen for an eternity, he got up.

He made his way over to the kitchenette in the back of the bookstore and poured himself another hot cup of tea.

He heard a knock on the front door and grimaced. He debated hiding in the back of the store until the person went away. But after several more aggressive knocks, he wandered toward the front of the store.

He almost jumped at the sight.

Eleanor Simmons, the pastor's sister had her tall thin frame pressed against the glass of the door, peering inside. Despite it being August in Mississippi, she was dressed all in black slacks, matching long sleeve shirt with ruffles and black stiletto heels. She had her hair pulled back in a severe bun that made her dark eyes even more menacing.

She was completely different than her brother, Pastor John.

Where Pastor John was warm and welcoming, she was stoic and cold.

He set down his tea on the counter and walked toward the front of the store.

As soon as he unlocked the door, she pushed her way inside. She looked over his shoulder and then back at him.

"Good morning, Eleanor. You know I'm not open now."

"It's Miss Simmons to you. And yes I know you're not open. Are you alone?" She lowered her voice and narrowed her eyes on him.

"As far as I know." He cocked his head wishing he'd brought Ringo into the bookstore with him today. Ringo would have run the rude woman out the second she tried to barge inside.

" I need to talk to you. I heard about you offering to be auctioned off as a date for charity."

"I didn't exactly offer…"

"It's a good business move for you. Money talks you

know. And I have it on good authority that Missy really likes you. And she's willing to pay for that special date."

His back stiffened. "Mrs. Simmons, I haven't agreed…"

"I also know that Gabriela Jackson has been frequenting your bookstore. I know you're new here and don't know how things work, but let me give you some friendly advice. Steer clear of her. If you align with her you will be shooting yourself in the foot when it comes to running your business."

His gut twisted. "I keep hearing how bad Gabriela is but no one is really willing to talk about what exactly she did that was so bad."

"I'm just giving you some friendly advice." Her smile slid off her face.

"Can I offer you some tea?"

"No. I don't drink tea." She grimaced and headed for the door. She cast a glance over her shoulder. "Just heed my warning"

The bell dinged as the door closed. He stepped forward and locked the door.

He stared out the window, watching Eleanor slink away like a black mist.

CHAPTER 8

Gabriela stood ten feet from the hive. Despite having the bee keepers suit on she still didn't feel protected from the insects.

"I don't think you really need me to help you look in the hive, Aunt Agnes." Another bead of sweat rolled down her neck to the waist of her jeans. "I don't even know what I'm looking for."

"That's why I'm here to teach you." Agnes quipped. "Now come over here to the hive. I'm going to get you to lift the lid and place it on the ground."

"But won't that make the bees mad? I mean I don't like people invading my privacy." She blinked away a bead of sweat that rolled from her forehead into her eye. She could feel her mascara running down her cheek.

"That's why you have to be nice about it." Agnes lowered the veil on her hat. She didn't even bother putting on a bee suit. She said she and the bees had an understanding.

The only understanding they could possibly have was that Agnes was nuttier than a fruit cake.

"Come on. I don't have all day." Agnes waved her forward.

Gabriela stiffened her spine and took a step toward what she felt like was an impending disaster.

With shaking hands she lifted the lid off the hive and slowly lowered it to the ground.

When she stood, Agnes was staring at her.

"What?"

"You always move that slow?" Agnes narrowed her eyes.

"When bees are involved, yes." Gabriela blinked through the sweat rolling down her forehead.

"Now we are going to check on the queen."

Gabriela peered down into the buzzing hive full of bees. Some had taken flight and were flying around their heads. The sound was almost deafening. Or maybe it the fear that was deafening.

"How can you tell who the queen is? There are so many bees." Gabriela shook her head.

"She's bigger than the other bees. Longer." Agnes pulled out a frame covered in honeycomb and bees. "She's not on this one. But it's good to check each frame to make sure there are no mites. This one is good."

Gabriela stayed as still as possible waiting and watching as Agnes pulled out each honey covered frame and examined them. On the middle one she pointed her boney finger to the middle of the honeycomb. "See, there's the queen."

Gabriela leaned in slightly. "She is bigger. I guess that's how they know she's in charge."

"She's in charge of laying all the eggs."

"Figures. The men get all the fun and the queen has to do all the labor. Sounds like bees are a lot like humans." Gabriela sighed.

Agnes shook her head. "I think they're better than humans. They each have a job and do it. They don't get mixed up in problems or complications. They do their job and then they eventually die."

"Sounds divine." Gabriela deadpanned. "So do you have mites or no?"

"Good news is we don't have mites."

"Perfect. Can I go?"

"Not yet. Hand me that jar over there and we'll harvest some of the honey."

Gabriela reached for the glass jar that Agnes had brought out of the house with her. She unscrewed the top and held out the jar.

"Now hold still." Agnes instructed. She pulled a knife out of the pocket of her overalls and cut some honeycomb off a frame. She placed it in the jar. A couple of bees followed the honey into the jar.

"How do I get the bees out?"

"They'll fly out as you walk farther away from the hive."

Gabriela nodded and took a few steps toward the house. By the time she made it to the front steps all the bees had come out of the jar and none were flying around her white bee suit.

Taking a deep breath and blowing it out she screwed the lid on the glass jar and set it on the steps of the front porch. She glanced over her shoulder making sure Agnes didn't need her help. The old woman had put the lid back on the hive and was walking toward her.

Gabriela got out of the suit as quick as she could.

She caught a glimpse of her reflection in glass of the front door.

She looked like a hot mess. Hair sticking up, mascara running and face red from the unbearable heat.

"See now, wasn't that fun." Agnes gave her a cheerful smile.

Gabriela stared at the woman.

"Well, why don't you go on inside and get cleaned up.

Then you can run this honey over to Colin at the English Rose."

"Again?" She propped her hands on her hips. "I already took him a ton of jars a few days ago."

"Yes again. He's sold all of those. He's out."

'Who is he selling those to? Why don't people in Harland Creek just come straight to you to buy their honey. He's probably jacking up the price to make a big profit." She swiped the back of her hand across her forehead.

"People in Harland Creek do come to me directly. But Colin is selling this honey online." Agnes shook her head at Gabriela, as if she didn't have a brain cell in her head.

"So why don't you sell it yourself online."

"'Cause I don't know a thing about online selling. I got enough to do as it is without having to worry about payment, packaging and shipping. If you want a shower before heading over to Colin's I suggest you be quick about it. Otherwise I'll be using the truck and you'll have to walk."

That got Gabriela's attention. It was one thing to walk at night but to walk five miles into town in the Mississippi heat was quite another.

She bounded up the stairs. "I'll be ready in twenty minutes."

CHAPTER 9

*G*abriela finished drying her hair and glanced at her reflection in the mirror.

She'd thrown on some cut off denim shorts and a white wrinkled T-shirt. She even skipped putting on makeup except for some pink lip gloss. She quickly threw her hair up in a messy bun and headed down stairs.

She poked her head in the kitchen looking for her aunt. She spotted the jar of honey with a note beside it.

She walked over and picked up the note.

"Gone with Elizabeth to pick up some fabric for the quilt. Take my pickup and deliver that honey to Colin. And don't flirt with him!"~ A

"Like I would even consider flirting with that stick in the mud" She snorted and grabbed the honey and keys to the pickup.

She shoved her sunglasses over the bridge of her nose and slid into the driver's seat of the old truck. The back of her legs stuck to the warm vinyl. She hissed and quickly started the engine and turned the air conditioning on full blast.

Barely any air came out and it was nowhere near cold.

"Figures." She muttered and rolled down the hand crank on the window. She managed to get the old seatbelt latched and put the truck in drive.

She barely had time to enjoy the drive before she was pulling onto the square. She spotted a parking spot in the front of the English Rose Bookstore and pulled in. She turned the engine off and the truck backfired and set up a plume of smoke.

So much for getting in and out of town without getting notice.

She grabbed the jar of honey and her bag and slid out of the truck. She didn't bother taking the keys with her or locking it. Everyone knew Agnes's truck and no one would dare try to steal it.

She noticed the Closed sign on the bookstore and frowned.

She tried the door. It wasn't locked.

Perfect. She would leave the honey and slip out without having to face the judgmental Colin.

She'd about had a heart attack when he found her out by the cliff overlooking the lake. Since she'd been back in town she'd gone out there every night.

It was her way of paying penance for her sin.

Not that she'd ever get rid of that stain. People didn't forget nor did they forgive. She couldn't imagine what the good Lord thought of her.

She would have that sin with her for the rest of her life.

She stepped inside and carefully closed the door behind her.

"Hello? I'm here to rob you of all your English tea and hardback classic novels." She waited. When no one answered she set the jar of honey on the counter and started to leave.

But an opened box of books caught her eye.

She glanced outside making sure no one was coming in. she walked over to the table and peered into the box.

She gasp with joy.

She carefully picked up one of the leather bound books. They were new and each book was a different color. Best of all they were all classics.

She held up the pink leather bound book of Heidi.

She carefully turned the pages, marveling at the beautiful illustrations.

She picked up another and bit her lip.

Charles Dickens A Christmas Carol.

She felt the smile stretch across her face.

"Can't you read?" Colin thundered behind her.

She jumped, nearly dropping the book. When she recovered her composure she turned and glared at him.

"Are you crazy? Do you usually go around scaring woman?"

"I didn't mean to scare you….Hey wait a minute. You're not supposed to be nosing around in my shop. The sign clearly says closed." He glared.

"And the door clearly wasn't locked. It's a free country, Downton Abby. You can't just go around leaving your place of business unlocked. You never know who might be sneaking in to look at your….goods." She arched her brow.

He sighed and flipped the sign around to Open. "What are you doing here?"

"Dropping off more honey." She frowned and set the book back in the box. "Aunt Agnes says you are selling her honey online."

"Yes. Readers tend to like honey in their tea. Her honey is the best around."

"How much are you making off my Aunt?" She narrowed her eyes.

"Making off your aunt? I'm buying it from her. You act like I'm stealing it." He looked offended.

"She's old and doesn't understand business. She should be selling it herself. To make more of a profit."

"So why don't you help her with it?" Colin shrugged. "You're young I bet you could whip up a website in no time. You did pretty good with making those labels for the honey jars for Alexandria's wedding."

"Don't remind me of that horrid event."

She'd agreed to help with the wedding simply because Alexandria was Olivia's friend. Olivia had been one of the few people in town who'd been decent to her since she arrived back in town. But Alexandria turned out to be a selfish arrogant woman who ended up marrying a womanizer.

Gabriela hoped she would get what was coming to her.

"I heard it was quite a show."

"Yeah, why didn't you show up. You provided English tea for the gift bags. Don't tell me she didn't invite you to the wedding."

"I had something else already planned for that day. Besides it wasn't like I knew her." He shrugged.

"Me either."

"Yes but you were also the wedding photographer. You had to be there."

"Yes I did." She smiled remembering how the photos had turned out. Half the wedding party pictures had an entitled family dog pooping in the background. Gabriela felt like it was karma since Alexandra had treated Olivia so poorly.

"Why are you smiling?" His eyes narrowed.

"No reason." She sobered. "I have to be going." She headed for the door.

"Stop"

Usually she didn't obey but something in his tone had her turning. "What?"

"Just a warning that I don't appreciate people handling my merchandise when I'm not here." He nodded toward the box of newly arrived books.

"Easy, Downton Abby. I'm not interested in your merchandise. " She gave him a saucy smile. The bell over the door dinged as she walked out the door, leaving him alone in his bookstore.

CHAPTER 10

*G*abriela's name seemed to be on everyone's mind that day.

Pastor John had popped in at lunch to pick up a set of Bible commentaries he'd ordered. While he was ringing him up, Pastor John mentioned that Gabriela had a great idea with the auction date.

Then Donna Williams had stopped by to inform him that the quilting group would miss the next two Thursdays of quilting. She mentioned how Gabriela sure looked tired and she was worried about the girl.

He started to say that if she wouldn't trespass and stay out so late every night the she'd be more than rested. But he stopped himself from spilling the beans.

He spotted Farmer Joe Smith walking his pig around the square when he came out of the country clerk's office. Farmer Joe seemed upset that Gabriela had not suggested him to be auctioned off for a date. Farmer Smith said he was as single as they come and just because some fancy pants Englishman landed on this side of the ocean it was no reason to snub the other bachelors of the county.

Colin couldn't agree more but the pig caught the scent of pork from the BBQ truck and squealed and bucked until he broke the thin rope leash. The traumatized pig ran off down Main Street which quickly became gridlock with people trying to corral the pig so it could be caught.

He spotted Agnes in the grocery store after he stopped in to grab something to cook and he saw the glare she shot him. She started to make her way over to him at the cash register but Donna had stopped her to chat. He saw his escape and darted out the store and headed to his car.

As he pulled up to his cottage, he spotted Ringo waiting for him on the porch. The dog lifted his head and then slid into a stretch before sitting up straight to welcome him home with a tail wag.

"Hey boy. I got you a treat tonight." He rubbed the dog's head and unlocked his house. They walked in and headed into the kitchen.

Ringo sat waiting patiently as he put away the small amount of groceries he'd purchased.

He pulled out a bag of dog biscuits and shook the sack.

Ringo licked his lips as his tail thumped loudly.

He opened the bag and pulled out a treat and handed it to him.

Ringo snatched the treat out of his hand and Colin winced. "You need better manners. One day you're going to take a finger off.'

Ringo trotted off to sit in front of the large living room window to eat his treat.

Colin sighed and glanced at the time. He had time to marinate the steak he'd bought and check on some online orders.

Usually he did all that at the bookstore but with the influx of new inventory and errands he had run, he didn't have time.

He glanced at the parcel sitting on his kitchen counter. It had arrived two weeks ago and he would have opened it except the return address was marked England.

He had managed to avoid it until now.

He grabbed a knife and slid it under the tape. He pulled open the lid and set it aside.

The box was full of foam popcorn.

He frowned as he dug around the box until his hand hit something glass. He pulled it out.

It was a bottle of expensive champagne with a note attached.

He set the bottle down and opened the letter. A sonogram picture fell to the floor. He forced his eyes to read the note

"We're having a baby! You're going to be an uncle!"~ Charles

He sunk down into the chair.

So his brother Charles and new wife, Margaret were going to have a baby.

Funny how last year he would have been overjoyed at the news of her having a baby.

But last year she was with him, and not his brother Charles.

Now, it hurt.

He studied the champagne, wanting to open it up and drown his painful past.

But he knew all it would do was make things worse. Since moving to Harland Creek he'd promised himself he would deal with his emotions instead of burying them in alcohol.

He set the bottle in the cabinet above the sink.

He would re-gift it when someone in town got married. Heather Smith and Grayson McCade had been dating pretty heavily since she moved to town. But if he had to bet on who would get married next, he would wager it would be Sam and Olivia.

Sam had loved Olivia as long as he had known her. Apparently the one who hadn't seen it was Olivia herself.

That changed after Alexandra's wedding.

The two friends who'd grown up together were now the talk of the town.

He had been happy for Olivia. The shy florist had been more than welcoming when he moved to Harland Creek. They had got on well. Probably because they were both very private people and preferred not to broadcast their news all over town.

Ringo let out a howl.

He headed over to the window and looked out.

A couple of deer were walking across the front yard in the direction of the tree line. They were headed to the lake.

"Hush boy. They're just out for a stroll. Come on in the kitchen while I get dinner started."

The dog obeyed and followed him into the kitchen.

He put the kettle on the stove and turned the heat on.

Lately he'd been having a cup of tea as he cooked.

He pulled out the fresh cut of steak for him and chicken breast for Ringo and laid it on the platter to season.

Ringo laid down and rested his face on his paws as he watched him work. He pulled the tiny bottles of seasoning out of the cabinet and some Worcestershire sauce out of the refrigerator.

He quietly worked with the dog at his feet.

It was nights like this that he enjoyed.

No drama, just quiet reflection and work.

"Woof." Ringo walked over to the window and looked out.

"What is it boy?" He hadn't heard anyone drive up. He quickly washed and dried his hands before going to the window and peered out. He saw Gabriela park her aunt's truck at the end of his driveway and get out. He waited to see if she were going to walk up to his house or disappear toward the river but instead she walked to the back of the truck.

She picked something up covered in a towel. Her arms were full as she walked to the tree line.

She stumbled and almost lost her balance but recovered.

Grumbling he opened the door and walked out with Ringo on his heels.

"What are you doing?"

She didn't seem surprised to see him. She started to give a sharp retort but when her gaze landed on Ringo her eyes widened. "Don't let that dog near me."

"Ringo? He wouldn't hurt a fly." Colin scowled, offended at her assumption.

Just then a little head peered out of the blanket and let out a cry.

"That' s a deer."

"Actually genius, it's a fawn." She kept her gaze trained on Ringo. "And I don't want your dog to hurt it."

"What are you doing with a fawn?"

She shifted the weight of the deer in her arms and grimaced. "I found it on the side of the road not far from here. I stopped and waited for the mother to come get it. But there was too much traffic and I was scared he'd get hit. So I'm bringing him here to see if she'll get it."

"Here let me hold it." He walked closer and Ringo followed. She looked unsure. "Ringo stay." He ordered the dog.

Ringo sat down and watched them with interest.

The fawn let out a cry.

"Have you seen any deer around here lately?" She let him take the fawn.

"Yes, a couple just came out of the tree line. Maybe he

belongs to one of them?" He walked over to the trees and Gabriela followed.

"Or maybe not? What if his mama doesn't come back? What if she got hit by a car? What do baby deer eat?"

He grinned at her rapid fire questions.

"I'm serious. I can't just let him die." She worried her lip with her teeth.

"Let's not get ahead of ourselves. First let's put the deer here. With all his crying, I'm sure the mom will hear him and come out."

The deer let out another cry.

"Poor thing. I tried to give him some blueberries I had in the truck but he didn't eat it. And he tried to nurse my neck when I picked him up." She looked defeated.

"Well if the mom is anywhere in the areas, she is sure to hear him." He bent and gently placed the fawn on the grass near a large tree. He stood and folded up the towel.

"Come on, let's wait inside the house and see what happens." He gently took her elbow.

Ringo walked over and sniffed the deer who let out another cry.

She gasped and took a step forward. He held her back.

"It's okay. He's just trying to figure out what it is. Ringo come."

Ringo gave the deer one last sniff and walked over to them. He stood beside Gabriela and gave her hand a lick.

She finally let him lead her into the house but she kept her gaze glued on the fawn the whole time. Once inside she stood at the window.

"You know the mother deer is probably waiting until you move away from the window before she steps out." He shook his head and walked into the kitchen.

She slowly knelt down until only her eyes were seen through the window.

Ringo sat beside her and cocked his head.

He smiled. "I didn't know you were such an animal lover."

"Don't go falling in love, Downton Abby. I have a reputation to protect as a cold hearted villainess." She glanced over her shoulder at him. "You should put me in your book. I make a fantastic bad guy."

"But what would I call you?" He turned the meat over and seasoned it. "Veronica?"

"Nah. I knew a Veronica in New York. She was too tender hearted. You need a name that will put fear into the hearts of men." She looked back out the window.

"Scarlet perhaps?" He quipped.

"Perhaps. Oh I see some movement in the tall grass by the trees." She pressed her face to the glass.

He frowned and wiped his hands off to join her at the window.

She grabbed his hand and pulled him to the floor. He landed with a thump.

"What are …."

She slammed her hand across his mouth. "You're going to scared the mama away." She scowled at him.

They stayed there like that, her hand on his mouth, her eyes blazing into his. And suddenly he realized the air conditioner must be out. The room got hot all of a sudden.

He slowly removed her hand. Her mouth parted slightly. Her eyes dilated.

She narrowed her eyes and tugged away.

Ringo stood and walked between them and gave her a lick on the cheek.

"Eww. I probably have rabies now." She wiped the kiss off with the back of her hand.

"You get rabies from a bite not a lick." He arched his brow.

"Aren't you a font of knowledge, Downton Abby." She deadpanned.

"Stop calling…."

She jerked her head toward the window. "Wait. Look." She pointed.

He followed her gaze outside.

A deer slowly made her way out from the grove. The fawn sat huddled on the ground crying out. The deer froze and then spotted her baby. She rushed over and bent her head. The baby got to its feet and began nursing.

Gabriela grabbed his hand. "It's happening. They found each other again." She squeezed his hand.

He turned. Her face was brilliant and beautiful. Far from the ice queen the town had branded her as.

He covered her hand in his and patted it. "Everything worked out. I told you not to worry."

She slowly tore her gaze away from the animals and looked at him. She frowned, suddenly realizing they were holding hands. She pulled out of his grasp and stood.

"I should go."

"You can't." He pointed out the window. The fawn was still feeding. "If you go out the door you'll scare the mom and she'll run off again. Let the fawn finish nursing first. That way she'll have the strength to follow mom back."

Frowning she looked at the deer. Her expression shifted. The veil of guardedness came down over her face.

The ice queen was back.

"Don't worry. I'll try not to fall in love with you in the brief time you are here." He snorted and walked back into the kitchen. "I would invite you to stay for dinner but I don't have enough food." He covered the steak and chicken with some foil and walked onto the back deck.

He was a little surprised she followed him onto the deck.

He figured he needed to treat Gabriela very much like

that wild deer in the front yard. Neither of them trusted humans.

"You have steak and chicken. You are eating all that yourself?" She arched her eyebrow. "Better watch out or you'll get chubby and lose the interest of the single young ladies in town."

"I have a high constitution." He patted his stomach.

"Try a laxative. That should help." She crossed her arms and leaned against the railing of the fence.

"I have a feeling you know what constitution means. You're just trying to irritate me."

"Is it working?" She looked hopeful.

"No. I'm not easily irritated." He shot back.

"I'll try harder." She lifted her chin.

He couldn't suppress a grin. He had an idea she meant every word.

"You know the bookstore has a studio above it. You could live there and save some money on buying a house."

"I prefer my privacy. Besides money's not an issue." He fired up the grill.

"Is that right? Well keep that info to yourself. Missy is looking to land a rich husband. She needs someone to pay off her credit card debt." She shoved off the railing and looked out over the backyard. "She has a penchant for shopping."

"So why are you here?"

"To bring the fawn back to its mother."

"No. Why are you here in Harland Creek. You certainly don't seem to like it very much. Besides I know models make a lot of money."

"Ha. I have it on good authority that models do not make a load of money. It's hard work with long hours and photographers sweating all over you, wanting you to always take another piece of your clothes off." She wrapped her arms around herself. "The money I did make I had to pay outrageous rent in New York."

"So why don't you model somewhere else? California or Europe." He walked back into the kitchen and grabbed the platter of meat.

"Because the agency I worked for black balled me. No one will touch me."

"Why did they do that? Think you were too difficult to work with?" He smirked.

Her face grew pale. She said nothing.

He put the meat on the grill and lowered the lid. "Gabriela. Answer the question."

"Why should I?"

"Because you kind of owe me. Pastor John expects me to be auctioned off for charity. I didn't have the heart to tell him or Wilma that I couldn't do it."

She sighed and shook her head. "All you have to do to get around that is tell them to open the auction up to phone in offers too. If you say money is no option then just ask someone to phone in an outrageous bid that no one can beat."

"That's...that's actually brilliant." He nodded feeling the weight he'd been carrying around lift.

"You're welcome." She walked over and patted his chest. "I'll be seeing you around."

She headed inside for the front door. He hurried after her and grabbed her hand.

"Wait."

She turned around and scowled. "What?"

He struggled to come up with a reason for her to stay. "The deer. Don't scare them off."

She pulled out of his grip and looked over at the window. She smirked and looked back at him.

"They are already gone. No reason for me to stay." She lifted her chin.

Ringo walked over and looked over at her and gave a whimper.

She looked down and smiled. "Aww you're a cutie when you're not drooling all over me."

'I bet you say that to all the guys." He quipped.

"Ohhh. Nice one, Downton." She gave him a smile of approval. "I'll see you around."

He watched her walk down his steps and over to the old pickup she'd arrived in. She slid inside, cranked the engine and drove away.

He put his hand on his chest and rubbed the spot near his heart. Suddenly overcome with a feeling of homesickness.

Sensing his change in demeanor, Ringo licked his hand.

Weird, he'd not felt homesick since he moved. Now it hit him all of a sudden.

Maybe it was opening the package? Or reading the note his brother had sent?

It certainly wasn't because of Gabriela. Surely not. He shook his head and walked back to the porch to finish his dinner for one with a canine companion.

CHAPTER 11

*G*abriela stormed into the kitchen with a handful of receipts and a shoe box. "Are you crazy, Aunt Agnes?"

"Well not officially. Although Dr. Derek tried to put me on some female pills one time for 'fits of rage', but I refused." Agnes shrugged.

"I'm not talking about your normal disposition. I'm talking about how you have all your receipts stuffed in a shoe box. How do you keep up with expenses and how much you are making?"

"Well if I can pay my bills for the month then it's a good month." Agnes took a sip of her coffee. "I don't required much to live on."

Gabriela stared back at her in disbelief. The old woman had probably lost thousands of dollars due to careless book-keeping.

"It's more than just paying your bills. You need to be organized. Know how much you have going on in expenses, how much coming in. What do you write off on taxes as expenses?"

Agnes frowned her wrinkles deepening. "Well, I had to buy a new queen bee a few years ago so there's that. And my mason jars for the honey."

"You can write off your vehicle. In fact, you should just buy a new one and write it off on your taxes."

"I don't think you can do that. "

"Of course you can. You need to treat your business like a business. And why are you letting Colin have the honey for less than what you normally charge?"

"Because he's such a nice young man." Agnes smiled.

"It's his accent isn't it? I know how much you just love Sean Connery." Gabriela narrowed her eyes.

Agnes set her coffee cup down on the table. "Don't get smart with me, young lady. And don't be bringing Colin into this. You just steer clear of him."

"Believe me, I don't want your fancy pants Englishman." She curled her hands into fists.

"Oh and Pastor John called. He wants you to come along today to help check on the progress of the silent auction items we've gotten so far. And he doesn't know how to actually advertise Colin for a date."

"You know, Aunt Agnes, you could be making more money if you had your own website. You could sell directly to people."

"I don't know anything about a website. I don't even have a computer. Plus there's the shipping and I don't know how to calculate all that. Sounds like a lot of trouble." Agnes shrugged and stood from the table.

Sometimes Gabriela wanted to strangle her aunt.

"Get something decent on. You can't go into the church wearing shorts." She stood from the table and rinsed out her coffee cup in the sink.

"Fine. I'll go put on a cocktail dress." She sat the shoebox of receipts on the table.

"Jeans will be fine. We're just going to help, not worship." Agnes quipped.

Gabriela sighed. "Fine. Give me ten minutes."

Thirty minutes later, they were standing in the fellowship hall. All the ladies from the quilting circle were there, along with Olivia McCade and Stacey Landers from Bettie's Boutique.

"Agnes, Gabriela, I'm glad you are here. Would you mind having a look at all the items for the auction and let me know how to set it out." Olivia rushed over to them and frowned. "I've never helped with one of these before and have some questions."

"She's your girl." Agnes jerked a finger in Gabriela's direction. "I'll be over chatting with Elizabeth over a piece of her famous coffee cake and coffee." She toddled away.

Gabriela glared. "Figures."

"Still not getting along with Agnes?" Olivia gave her a sympathetic look.

Gabriela felt herself relax a little as she turned to the only kind person in Harland Creek.

"We've always had a love hate relationship." Gabriela deadpanned. "She hates it when I show up and loves it when I leave."

Olivia grinned and shook her head. "You can always come over to my house.' She patted her arm.

Gabriela smiled. "Thanks but I don't think Sam would like that very much. Mooching in on his time with you."

Olivia ducked her head and blushed.

"So when are you two getting married?" Gabriela arched her brow.

Olivia blushed deeper. "I don't know. Everything has been so busy and well he's not asked me yet."

"You'll get married before Heather and Grayson do."

"I doubt that." Olivia shook her head. "They've been dating longer."

"Yeah but you and Sam have been together longer. Even if the majority of that time was just friends. My money is on you guys getting married first."

"We'll see. All I can say is that I'm glad we started dating before this auction date came up. I can't imagine having to watch Sam up there being bid on by all the single women in Harland Creek." Olivia shook her head.

"Yeah." Gabriela cut her eyes over to Colin who was standing beside Missy Long who had just arrived. From the looks of things they were deep in conversation. He was leaning down to listen to whatever it was she was saying.

"So how do you like Colin? "

"He's okay for a stuck up English man." She tore her gaze away from them and looked at the table of items to be auctioned.

"I think he's lovely. I also think he moved here to escape from a broken heart in England." Olivia sighed softly.

Gabriela jerked her head over to Olivia. "Did he tell you that?"

"No but the few conversations I've had with him, he kind of hinted." Olivia shrugged. "I mean I can't imagine anyone breaking his heart. I kind of thought it would be the other way around."

"He's not that good looking, Olivia. I mean yeah he's tall and sophisticated with a British accent. He's not like the other guys around here."

"That's exactly what makes him cute."

"Distinguished. I'll give him distinguished but not cute." Gabriela crossed her arms and studied Colin from across the room. "He's a horrible dresser I mean look at those ugly shoes."

Colin looked up at her at that moment.

She straightened and glanced away feeling her face flame.

"I think he knows we are talking about him." Olivia whispered.

"Then let's get busy looking at the auction items." Gabriela grabbed her arm. Together they walked down the line of items.

"I would start each item with a written bid. People aren't going to bid first. So just write in a dollar amount and state on the ticket that bids should increase by the dollar. Just to keep things easy and moving."

"Great idea." Olivia jotted a note down on her clipboard. "What about how things are set up?"

"Why don't you arrange things in groups? Home décor, clothing, food items.... Just to keep things orderly."

"Perfect. Anything else?"

"Yes. Make sure each auction item has its own pen. You won't believe how pens walk off in something like this."

Olivia nodded and looked up. "Oh, Donna is waving me over. Looks like she has some other items that someone just dropped off." She smiled and gave Gabriela's arm a gentle squeeze. "I'll see you late."

"Will do." Gabriela nodded.

"Oh and Gabriela. If you are interested in Colin you should go ahead and make your intentions clear." Olivia grinned as she walked away leaving Gabriela looking quite like a trout.

"She's clearly lost her mind." Gabriela mumbled.

"Who has lost their mind?" Colin appeared beside her.

Gabriela felt her face go red. "Olivia."

"I won't stand to hear a bad word about Olivia. She was the first friendly face to welcome me to Harland Creek."

"You and me both, Downton Abby." Gabriela lifted her chin. "You'll never hear me say a bad word about Olivia." She cut her eyes at him and then across the room. Missy was staring her down

Gabriela smirked. "Your girlfriend is upset that you are talking to me. You should go reassure her that there's nothing untoward going on." She spoke the last words with a strong British accent.

"Missy is not my girlfriend. She's just a friend." He lifted his chin.

Gabriela laughed out loud. "Then you should probably make that clear to her. "

"Gabriela, Colin. I'm glad to see you both here." Pastor John joined them. He smiled and clasped his hands together.

"Hello Pastor John." Gabriela and Colin spoke in unison.

"I'm hoping we can get the final details worked out about this auction date. I like to be prepared so we an iron out any problems ahead of time." Pastor John nodded.

"I can't imagine any issues with a date bought from an auction." Colin sighed heavily.

Gabriela shook her head. "You could advertise in the Jackson paper? It would certainly draw in more people."

"I'm not comfortable with that idea. You never know what kind of crazy person might win" Colin narrowed his brows together.

"You're right. There are plenty of crazy people right here in Harland Creek. No need to transport them in." Gabriela sighed.

Pastor John swallowed and shifted his weight, clearly uncomfortable in taking part in that conversation.

"Do we need a sign-up sheet for the auction, like we are doing for the rest of the items?" The Pastor asked.

Gabriela grinned. "Actually, what I would do is have an emcee lead the auction. Have Colin stand on the stage, you know show off the merchandise."

Colin cringed. But she didn't miss a beat.

"You need someone who has the gift of gab who would get people to bid. You basically want a bidding war."

"An emcee?" Pastor John rubbed his chin.

"Yeah someone who can get the bid up."

"I think I might know someone. Let me talk to her first." Pastor John nodded and walked away.

"An emcee? You might as well slap a blue ribbon on me, put a rope around my neck and parade me around the room like a cow."

"Actually you would be a bull since you're a man." She pointed her finger in his face. "And don't tempt me. I think Aunt Agnes has an old cow bell out in her barn that she used to keep on her milking cow. It would match your pretty green eyes." She batted her eyes at him.

"Stop that. You're making people stare." He muttered under his breath.

"Sorry. Forgot you are trying to keep your reputation lily white." She took a step away from him.

"Stop being so dramatic." He stepped closer to her.

She frowned at him. "Stop standing so close. You're going to give Missy the wrong idea about us. And you are ruining your chances of her wanting to bid on you."

"I don't want her to bid on me." He groused.

"Yeah? Well you could do worse. I can name off a lot of other women in town who have their eyes set on you."

Who?" He frowned.

"Stacey for one."

"Stacey Landers? How do you know that? It's not like she'd talk to…."

She stiffened. "It's not like she'd talk to me. Isn't that what you were going to say?"

"I didn't mean…"

"Oh stop trying to talk your way out of this. Besides it's true. The last time I talked to Stacey she was telling me I wasn't welcome inside her boutique and I couldn't stand on the sidewalk because I was loitering. And loitering was a crime."

Colin blinked. "She actually said that?"

"Yeah."

"People loiter on the sidewalk all the time. This is a small town. Everybody does it." He frowned looking very confused.

"And I'm not other people. I'm Gabriela Jackson. The harlot of Harland Creek." She arched her brow.

"Gabriela…"

"So let's discuss how this auction should be done." She brushed off his question and quickly changed the subject.

"What's there to discuss?" He rolled his eyes.

"Well for one," She whipped out a small notebook and pen from her purse, "we need to advertise for this event. We only have a week to go and it's important to push this as much as we can."

"I'd rather not be plastered across every newspaper and social media page from here to Tennessee." He scowled.

She bit her lip and studied him. "Okay. I'll handle the publicity. Next thing I need from you is a profile picture and a write up."

"A write up?"

"Yes. A bio. I need to get your history, where you are from, your hopes and dream, what hobbies you enjoy?" She poised her pen to write.

"Is that really necessary?"

"Fine. Can you at least give me your name and what part of England you are from?"

"Colin Bennet. London England." He crossed his arms.

"Middle name?" She tapped her pen on the paper.

"Rutherford."

"Really?" She cringed.

He uncrossed his arms and glared down at her. "It's a family name."

"It would have to be wouldn't it?" She sighed.

"What's your middle name?" He smirked.

"None of your beeswax. Next topic." She jotted down his full name. "Hobbies? Besides drinking tea and reading."

"I don't know. I haven't had much time to have any hobbies since I moved to town." He shrugged.

"Don't worry. I'll make something up."

He gave her a horrified look.

"Now, let's go over to the newspaper and we'll get a picture of you."

"A picture?"

"Yes. You need to let the public get a view of what they're buying. Come along now." She stuck her pen in her purse and hurried over to the pastor where she quickly gave him a run-down of where they were going.

The pastor seemed pleased that they were making such head way.

Colin, on the other hand, looked horrified.

CHAPTER 12

Colin slid into the old pickup truck as Gabriela got behind the wheel. When she closed the door, her floral perfume filled the cabin of the truck.

He felt his heart beat a little faster.

Probably because she couldn't drive.

She turned on the truck and threw it into drive. He jerked forward.

"You don't wear seatbelts where you come from?" She aimed a perfect eyebrow at him.

Sighing he reached around and fastened the seatbelt.

A few minutes later they were pulling into the parking lot of the Harland Creek Herald.

They got out and walked to the front door.

"I don't think I need a picture for this thing."

"I think you do. Pictures sell products. I should know."

She walked in and he reluctantly followed behind him.

"Where's Albert?" She asked the secretary sitting at her desk.

The older woman didn't bother looking up from reading

a romance novel as she answered. "In the break room." She licked her thick finger and used it to turn the page.

Gabriela's heels clacked down the hallway with purpose as she made her way down the hallway. Colin didn't miss the curious looks he got as he walked behind her. She pushed the glass door open to the room which housed a vending machine, coffee pot, beat up refrigerator and matching microwave and sink.

Albert looked up. A wide smile spread across his face when he spotted Gabriela.

He stopped eating potato chips and wiped his greasy fingers on his tan slacks. "Gabriela. I didn't expect to see you here."

"I know. Look I need to borrow your camera. "

"Again?" He frowned.

"Yes, again.' She propped her hand on her hip. "It's for him." She jerked her thumb in Colin's direction.

"For what? Is he getting married too?" His eyes widened.

"No. I assure you I am not getting married."

"It's for the charity event."

"I'm supposed to be taking pictures of the items being auctioned. Not you , Gabriela. Say, they're not paying you are they?" His eyes narrowed suspiciously.

"No. And if you are taking pictures of the items, then you need to take a picture of him. He's the one being auctioned off for a date." She crossed her arms.

His eyes grew wide. "So that wasn't a rumor?" He slowly stood.

"I'm afraid not.' Colin sighed wishing he were anywhere but here having this conversation.

"You know. A lot of people aren't happy about it." Albert lifted his chin.

"When you say a lot of people you mean you. You are a lot of people." Gabriela deadpanned.

"Well yeah. I mean I'm the town's bachelor. Never been married. I'm coming up on forty. I need a date." He crossed his arms and looked offended.

"I thought you had a thing for Denise. At the dollar store."

He went a bright red. "Where'd you hear that?"

"The whole town knows. It's common knowledge that she sneaks an extra candy bar into your bag when you check out. A candy bar that she pays for out of her pocket."

He blinked. "Really? I always thought it was buy one get one free."

Gabriela groaned. "Can I borrow your camera or not?" She grabbed Colin's wrist and looked at his watch. "You could let me borrow your camera while you run over to the dollar store."

He blinked rapidly as the wheels in his head spun. "Well, it's almost lunch time…"

"Yeah it is. So you better get going." Gabriela smiled.

He nodded and tossed his potato bag in the garage. "Come to my desk and I'll grab my camera."

Gabriela said nothing as she followed him. He grabbed his camera out of the drawer of his desk and handed it to her "Just be careful with it. It's very expensive."

"Will do. We'll walk over to the church and take some pictures near the cemetery."

Albert cringed.

"They have a pretty area in the back with flowers. Looks kind of like England." Gabriela took the camera and motioned for Colin to follow her.

He fell into step with her. He didn't have to slow his pace for her. Her long legs kept up with his long strides so they walked at an easy pace.

"Here. Let's go in by the back gate." She pointed to the wrought iron fence gate at the back of the church.

He reached around and unlatched the gate and waved her in first.

"Always the gentleman." She nodded. "That will come in handy on your date."

He gritted his teeth.

"What? No snappy comeback?"

"I'm fresh out."

"You probably need some lunch. After we get some pictures you should grab some lunch. I know I always feel better after eating."

"I didn't think models ate." He closed the gate behind them.

"Ha! See! You did have one more comeback in you.' She smiled broadly.

"Actually I was serious."

She pointed to an old oak tree. It's limbs were almost touching the ground. "Go stand by that tree. And try to look available."

He rolled his eyes and walked over to the tree. "I don't like having my photograph taken." He scowled.

"Why not? Don't you take pictures in England?" She checked her camera.

"Yes, but I'm not very photogenic. My brother is the good looking one." He shoved his hands in his pockets and studied the ground.

"Don't move." She ordered.

He started to look at her but she barked at him again.

"Freeze! Don't move a muscle." She quickly snapped a few shots.

He held his hands up. "But I wasn't even smiling."

"Women don't want you smiling. They want mysterious. That's what we're giving them, Downton."

He scowled at her nickname for him.

She snapped another picture.

"Don't you dare use that picture." He pointed his finger at her.

"Why not?" She studied the camera. "Women like broody. Although I'm not sure if you look moody or mysterious or constipated."

He grabbed the camera from her.

"Hey! Give it back."

"No. It's my turn to take your picture." He held the camera up.

She crossed her arms over her chest and shot daggers at him.

He snapped a picture and then looked at the image. "You need to smile more. Broody doesn't work on you."

She uncrossed her arms and rolled her eyes.

She shoved a strand of hair behind her ear and looked away.

He snapped a picture.

"Stop doing that." She shot him a glare.

"Give me one good picture and I'll stop."

"Fine." She leaned against the tree and stared at him.

He took her picture.

"Great now give it back." She held out her hand.

He handed the camera back to her.

"Come on and lean against the building. The brick will make your green eyes stand out in the picture."

He did as she asked. "You're the first person to notice my eyes are green and not blue."

"Well it's a subtle shade of green." She shrugged and stepped closer. With her fingertips, she fixed his hair.

He inhaled her scent. It was faintly sweet, with a hint of citrus, and not overpowering.

"My hair is fine." His voice turned to gravel.

"You need a haircut." She shook her head.

"I like it like this." He grabbed her hand.

65

Their gazes locked and the world went silent.

She stepped back. "I think we have enough pictures. Albert will email these to me."

"I didn't think you had a computer at your aunt's house."

"I don't. I'll use the computer at the library." She walked toward the gate.

"Just use the computer at the bookstore."

"You have a computer at the bookstore?" She looked at him over her shoulder.

"Yes. It's in the back near the fireplace. And it's for public use."

"That would be better. Plus I still have to write up a bio about you." She waited for him to latch the gate.

"Don't write anything stupid." He warned.

"Don't worry. I'll let you read it before I post it." She grinned sweetly. She looked past him and her smile dropped. "Oh no." She ducked behind a parked car on the side of the street.

"What are you…" Before he could finish, Travis was walking up towards him. He stepped forward a few feet to keep him from discovering her.

"Hey, Colin. I heard that Gabriela walked over here with you to the church." He glanced around and shifted his weight. "I was looking for her."

"We were at the church but she left. I think she headed toward the grocery store. To pick up some food…for her aunt." He was a horrible liar.

"Oh." He looked like he didn't believe him.

"I can tell her you were looking for her, if you want." Colin offered.

"No. No don't do that. She doesn't want to see me. I think in order to talk to her I'm going to have to surprise her."

"I don't think Gabriela would like that." Colin warned.

Travis laughed. "You know her then."

"Not really. " he shook his head.

"I'll head over to the grocery store to see if I can catch her." He lifted his hand and walked away.

He waited until Travis disappeared around the corner and then looked down at Gabriela.

'He's gone. You can come out now."

Gabriela stood, gripping the camera in her hand. "Thanks for not giving me away."

"I have a feeling you're not going to tell me what that was about."

"Nope."

"You owe me. That's the second time I've had to help you hide from that guy. Is he an old boyfriend?"

"You sure ask a lot of questions." Gabriela glared and started walking.

He quickly caught up. "I'm serious. You owe me one."

"If I agree, will you stop asking me about my past?" She quickened her pace. He matched her stride.

"Sure." He smiled.

"Fine. I owe you one. Now I need to get back to the farm so I can work on this auction."

"Perfect." He smiled and watched her walk away.

CHAPTER 13

*G*abriela parked far enough away from Colin's house that he wouldn't see her headlights. Aunt Agnes had ridden over to Wilma's house with Elizabeth to spend the night. Wilma's daughter had an emergency back home and had to head back to Jackson for the weekend. She'd asked some of the ladies to spend the night with her because she'd had chemotherapy that morning and she was feeling weak. Aunt Agnes and Elizabeth jumped at the offer to help.

Tonight not only was Gabriela on her own. She also had the use of the pickup truck.

She slid out of the truck and headed through the woods, the path she had memorized in her sleep.

Her throat tightened the further she walked. Her shoulders slumped with the weight of guilt.

She hated coming to this spot. But the self-destructive part of her that she couldn't shake woke her up every night to come here.

To make her remember.

So she'd never forget.

The night was pitch black so she'd been forced to bring a flashlight. The light bobbed along the ground and she kept stumbling along the muddy ground. Thankfully she'd worn her sneakers tonight instead of her sandals. The evening rain had made a mess of her deer path that she followed to the river.

She finally broke through the trees and slung her backpack on clump of green grass near the base of a tree.

She shined her flashlight across the expanse of the cliff and beyond to the lake below.

"You're trespassing again."

Colin's deep voice made her jump, her flashlight falling to the ground.

"You're going to give me a heart attack one of these days." She glared at him through the dark. She knelt down.

He aimed his flashlight on the ground where her flashlight had landed. She grasped it and stood.

"What are you doing here?" She scowled.

"I could ask you the same thing. And judging by the fact you still have your clothes on you aren't going skinny dipping." He shone the light on her backpack. "You having a picnic or something?"

"Something." She walked over to the tree and sat down. She pulled the backpack into her lap.

He didn't take the hint but instead sat down beside her.

"You're staying?"

"Well it is my land."

She stared at him in the dark feeling more vulnerable with him than with anyone she'd ever met.

She reluctantly pulled out a notebook and pen. He said nothing as she began to write.

She jotted down some words.

"Is this my bio for the auction date?"

"Not everything is about you." She shot back. When he

stayed silent she felt like she needed to relieve the tension between them.

"I'm coming up with an idea for Aunt Agnes for her business. She needs to be smarter in selling her honey and other items. Right now, she could do a subscription box that's mailed out every month or every three months. She could put a jar of honey, some beeswax candles, and some of her homemade soap. She makes different flavors so she could always have something different in her box."

"That's actually… a really good idea."

"I know. That's because I thought of it."

He shook his head. "But I can't imagine Agnes having enough time to put the boxes together."

"She can hire a senior from the high school . Because these are only sent out once a month or once a quarter it won't disrupt her routine."

"I saw her selling lip balm at the Founder's Day parade.'

"Yes. I knew I forgot to add that." She quickly jotted it down on the paper.

"Is Agnes excited out this?"

"She doesn't know yet."

"You've done an awful lot of work for something she might not be interested in."

"I know." She said softly. It was the part of her that was trying to make amends. If not to the town, at least to her own blood relative.

"She could include some of my English teas that I get shipped over. She would just pay me what I pay. I wouldn't make a profit."

She brightened. "Tea is perfect with honey." She jotted some more ideas down on her paper.

He leaned against the tree letting her do her work without interrupting. In a way it was soothing.

All her life people had always badgered her for her attention. To them, she seemed like some ethereal unattainable being. She'd often wished she could escape somewhere deep into the forest where she could breath.

She'd been the belle of the ball until that one tragic night.

Then she'd become a pariah. In a strange ways, he'd gotten her wish.

"Travis came by the bookstore again looking for you.'

She sighed suddenly the weigh to reality crashing in on her. "You really should just tell him that you have no idea where I am and that we are not friends. He'd probably quit hounding you then."

"Why does the town not seem to like you, Gabriela?"

The way he said the words were breathtakingly sad. She blinked and looked over at him. In the dark, she pictured him looking at her with those green eyes and longish nose. On someone else it would have looked odd, but on Colin it suited him. The accent helped as well.

"Colin…"

"Gabriela." He reached over and grabbed her hand. She tried to tug away but he held onto her gently. "Please. You kind of owe me you know."

"Why don't you ask one of the women in town? I'm sure Missy would be glad to tell you." She leaned back against the tree but didn't pull her hand out of his grasp. It was nice to have someone hold her hand that didn't want anything.

"Because I want the truth. That's why I'm asking you." He leaned back against the tree.

She could make out the outline of his face. He had his head tilted upward looking at the starry sky.

She did the same.

Then she took a deep breath.

CHAPTER 14

"They didn't always hate me you know." Her voice was low and sad.

Something twisted in his chest.

He wanted to say something, to comfort her and tell her she was wrong, but he didn't. He needed to hear what she had to say.

"I was the most popular girl in Harland Creek. There wasn't a day that went by that people weren't trying to get my attention or land in my good graces. All the girls wanted to be my friend and all the boys wanted to be my boyfriend."

"Sounds like you had it all."

"You would think that. But I can tell you that there were days when all I wanted was to escape to somewhere no one would find me. Just so I could be by myself and soak in the silence and dream about what I wanted in life."

He wanted to speak but didn't want her to end her train of thought so he remained silent.

"I discovered this place by accident." She waved her hand across his land. "In high school we always hung out at the lake but had never gone this far up. I found this by accident when my car broke down one night on my way home from the football game. I got out and figured I could ask Ms. Willis to call my dad. I got distracted when I was walking through the trees. Instead of going to Ms. Willis's house I kept going through the woods, entranced by the silent and peacefulness. When I broke through the trees I came out here. It was spring and there were tiny blue flowers everywhere. It was magical."

"I walked a little further to the cliff over there and looked down. The moon was casting its light on the water below making it sparkle like a thousand stars."

"Nice analogy." He simply said.

"Yeah, maybe I should be the writer." She deadpanned.

He chortled and then waited for her to continue her story. "So what did you do?"

"Well, I stayed as long as I could before running over to Ms. Willis's house to call my father. I didn't want to get in trouble for missing curfew." She shrugged. "After that night I started coming back here. I'd park off road where no one could see and take a blanket. I could lay out under the stars and just breath."

He nodded, understanding what she meant.

After a few brief seconds she cocked her head. "And then that one night that changed everything. Travis and his best friend Ricky had apparently seen me take this route home. Ricky had asked to take me to a bonfire that Missy's parents were having but I didn't want to go. It would be too noisy and I had grown addicted to my hidden spot here."

"So, like I had done many times before, I left the football game and headed over here. When I got here I put out my blanket and this time I brought a sleeping bag and pillow. I had told my mom that I was spending the night with Missy. Instead I was going to spend the night here."

"You weren't afraid?"

"I was never scared of the dark."

"Snakes?" He countered.

"It was too cold for snakes to be out." He could hear the amusement in her voice.

"Anyway I got here and set my stuff up and that's when I heard something in the woods. I've never been scared before until then."

"What was it?" He tightened his grip on her hand.

"It was Travis and Ricky. They'd followed me. They wanted to know what I was doing. And I said I came here for some peace and quiet. But they didn't get the hint. They wouldn't leave. Instead they started saying things to try to impress me. They said they were going to jump off the cliff. I told them that only an idiot would do that because it was such a long way down."

She shook her head and sighed. "I got mad because I knew they weren't leaving. So I got up and started gathering my things. That's when Ricky said he loved me and would do anything for me."

"I was shocked. I knew he liked me but he was the quiet shy guy who always got good grades. Truth be told I really liked him too but I knew he was bound for better things in life, like a scientist or doctor or some kind of inventor who would change the world. Ricky and Travis were totally different. Travis was more the outgoing macho type. Always outdoing the next guy."

"They didn't sound like they were very good friends. I'm surprised they were together that night."

"They weren't that good of friends. I think Ricky helped Travis a lot in school, you know on his papers and probably did some of his homework. I'm not sure why he did that."

"Then what happened?" He asked.

"I gathered my stuff ready to go when Ricky said he loved

me. Travis got angry and said that Ricky would never jump. The next thing I knew Ricky went over the cliff."

"But it's not very deep." Colin's stomach knotted.

"I must have screamed so loud that Ms. Willis heard me. She came running through the woods and found me crouched on the ground looking over the cliff. She dragged me back and all I kept saying was he went over the cliff. She called the cops. By dawn they found his body washed up on the shore."

"Oh my gosh. That's awful." He placed his other hand on top of hers.

"The cops got there and discovered my sleeping bag. They'd assumed I was there with him alone."

"Didn't you tell them about Travis being there?"

"I tried. They wouldn't listen. Finally one officer went to talk to him but he said he was there but left. He said he didn't see Ricky when he fell."

"He lied." Colin sat up.

She shrugged.

"After the investigation, they ruled it as an accidental death. They said he was probably showing off for me to get my attention." She shook her head. "By the time everything was finished, the whole town had blamed me for his death."

"But it was an accident. You had nothing to do with it."

"It didn't matter, Colin." She pulled out of his grasp. "People will believe what they want."

"So you'll let them believe a lie?"

She shook her head. "No. I tried getting Travis to tell them what happened but he wouldn't listen. He didn't talk to me after that."

"So what did you do?"

"I tried to find a way out as soon as I could. There was a modeling contest in Jackson and I entered. And won a contract to New York. As soon as my classes for my senior year were finished I left. I didn't even walk in graduation."

"So you just left?"

"It wasn't that hard to do. By that time, my parents had gotten the cold shoulder from the entire town. They were in real estate and had done very well. So as soon as I left they were looking to move. They ended up in Boca Raton. Aunt Agnes is my only family here."

"So why did you come back? You could have gone to Florida." He said gently.

"They actually didn't tell me they had moved. So when I arrived I found out from Agnes." She shrugged. "I did go to Boca to see them. But I didn't stay long. I seem to be a reminder of how they fell from high standing in Harland Creek. So I came back here. I'm hoping that if I can get this subscription box thing going for Aunt Agnes, she'll pay me. Just until I have enough money to go somewhere else."

"You don't have any money saved from modeling?"

" A little. And not enough to get me where I'm going."

"Where is that?" The thought of her leaving didn't sit well in his chest.

"Colorado or Wyoming. I'd like to help small businesses and make them more profitably. Maybe assess their store or website and build a plan how to sell more efficiently."

"No modeling."

"Only if I have to. You'd be surprised how many photographers think they have a right to your body while they are taking pictures.." She shook her head.

"Did someone hurt you?" Rage thundered through his chest and he leaned toward her.

"I can handle myself Colin." She reassured him

"You shouldn't have to. That's the point." He growled.

"Anyway, so that's my sad pitiful story. What's yours?"

He swallowed hard.

'Come on. It's only fair." She chided.

The moon had come out behind the clouds and her face was illuminated under the glow.

She was right. It was only fair. But somehow uttering the words only made his stomach churn.

CHAPTER 15

*G*abriela felt exposed. Having told Colin about her past, she couldn't hide behind her veneer of fake confidence where he was concerned. He knew too much.

"Well, are you going to tell me how you ended up in Harland Creek. Of all the places in the world I would think you could have chosen a more exciting place."

"I like small town Southern charm."

"You could have moved to Charleston. Or Memphis. Or Atlanta…"

"I wanted to go where no one could find me." He blurted out.

She stilled "I can understand that." She frowned. "You didn't kill anyone did you?"

"No, " He laughed. "Nothing like that."

"Then what's so bad that you want to disappear?"

"You……"

Ringo came running through the trees barking. He spotted Colin and piled into his lap licking him in the face.

"What's got you so excited, boy?" Colin laughed and held the dog at bay while trying to wipe the slobber off his face.

"Colin! Colin, where are you?"

Gabriella stilled at Missy's voice.

She pressed her finger to her lip to let Colin know not to alert Misty to their presence as she scrambled to her feet.

Just as she gathered her bag and flashlight, and stepped behind a large tree, Missy popped out of the woods and into the clearing.

Gabriela pressed her body against the rough bark of the tree.

"Colin what are you doing out here?" Missy shone her flashlight in his face.

He scowled and lowered her light. "I could ask the same about you."

Gabriela bit her lip.

"You know this place is haunted. The spirit of a boy still walks these woods. A boy that Gabriela killed." Missy lifted her hand.

Gabriela felt nausea rise in her throat but said nothing.

"Actually, that's not true. That story isn't how that poor boy died. She had nothing to do with it."

"Is that what she's been trying to tell you?" Missy looped her arm in his and leaned closer. "You need to watch yourself where Gabriela Jackson is concerned. She destroys lives."

"Well good thing I don't have much of a life to destroy."

Gabriela snorted.

Missy stiffened and then looked around. "Did you hear that?"

Gabriela closed her eyes and prayed for a miracle.

"It's probably a deer. They're out here a lot. Now let's walk back to the house and you can tell me what you are doing out here so late. Nothing's wrong is it?" Colin guide her back into the forest.

"No but I just wanted to talk to you about the auction date." Missy's voice grew fainter as they walked back to his house.

When she could no longer see the play of the flashlights or hear any voices, Gabriela sank to the ground in relief.

She would give them a good solid twenty minutes before venturing back to the truck. In the meantime, she enjoyed the solitude and the quiet of the night.

CHAPTER 16

"Get dressed." Agnes stuck her head in Gabriela's room.

Gabriela tried to pretend she was asleep.

"Gabriela, I'm serious. "

"Fine.' She threw the covers down and sat up. "Why do you need me to get up?"

"Because you have to help with the date that the auction is holding. And the pastor wants us to get the whole thing printed up and ready for the paper."

She sighed. "I already helped list all the items for auction."

"All except one." Aunt Agnes narrowed her eyes. "You need to get the whole write up about Colin ready."

"You're going to give me an ulcer.' She glared back and scrambled out of bed. "You don't have a computer so I'm going to have to go to the library to use their computer. Which means I need the truck."

"You can't have the truck. I have to go pick up my beehives from the apple orchid."

"Can't you do that tomorrow?"

"No. I'm on a schedule. That's a word you need to learn." Agnes snarked. "But I will do you a solid."

"Please don't attempt to use slang in your everyday conversation. It's just painful." Gabriela rubbed her temple.

"I'll drop you off in town on my way to the orchard."

She sighed. "When are you leaving?"

'In ten minutes."

Gabriela grabbed her clothes and headed for the bathroom. She took a quick shower and dressed. Forgoing makeup she pulled her hair up in a ponytail and slipped her feet into her sneakers.

She heard the truck engine start and her heart lurched.

She grabbed her backpack and her notebook and raced down the stairs.

Aunt Agnes had put the truck in reverse just as she hit the last step on the front porch.

She made it to the truck in time and scrambled inside.

She'd known since she was a little child that Agnes Jackson waited on nobody. When she was ready to go, she left. Even if she left you behind.

"You look nice" Her Aunt cast a look at her.

"It's just jeans and a shirt." She dug around in her bag looking for her sunglasses. While she didn't care much for expensive clothes, she loved her expensive sunglasses.

She finally found the Prada glasses and shoved them on over her eyes, shielding her from the glare of the morning sun.

"What are your plans for today?" Her Aunt turned onto the road leading into the heart of town.

"After I get this typed up and sent over to the newspaper, I was going work on this project I've started."

"Is it job related?"

"Yes. And that's all you need to know."

"I heard from one of the women in the quilting group that

one of the stores in Jackson is looking for a model to model their swimwear line. If you want I'll call up Donna and get the information…."

"No. Don't do that." She crossed her arms over her chest. "Why are you moving your hives?"

"Because the apple orchid doesn't need to be pollinated anymore and I need to get them over to Elizabeth's."

"Her flowers did really well this year."

'They did. That woman always had a green thumb."

"Heather certainly was a big help to her."

"Yes she is. I hope she continues to stay with her and help."

"Why wouldn't she stay? Harland Creek is her home now." Gabriela looked over at her Aunt.

"Yes, well, her and Grayson are getting very serious. I suspect he'll propose marriage pretty soon which means Heather will move out of Elizabeth's house and into Grayson's."

'Yes, but she'll always work there. She'll inherit the farm from Elizabeth." Gabriela frowned'

Aunt Agnes pulled onto the street where the library was located. "Yes well, Heather is young. And young people tend to get wild hairs and up and leave when they think things are getting too tough."

Gabriela swallowed She sensed the conversation wasn't about Heather at all but about her. "Heather grew up in the foster system. She knows tough times. She may be young. But she's seen the harsh reality of life. And now in Harland Creek she sees the beautiful side of life."

Aunt Agnes pulled up to the curb of the library. She put the truck in park and looked over at Gabriela. "You had the world by the tail, Gabriela…"

She had her hand on the door handle before her Aunt got halfway through her sentence. "Can't stay and chat. I've got to get going. " She opened the door and hopped out with her backpack slung across one shoulder.

Without looking back she hurried into the library where she could be shielded from the look of shame and disappointment from her Aunt.

CHAPTER 17

$\mathcal{C}$olin had just put the new leather bound book, Arabian Nights on the top self when the bell above the door tinkled.

"It's done. You are officially a commodity to be given to the highest bidder." Gabriela sauntered in and slung her backpack on the counter.

"The way you say it makes it sounds so humiliating. Did you come in here to use the computer?"

"No I used the library computer." She brightened. "I sent in your bio to the paper so you should get a glimpse in tomorrow's edition."

He put his hand to his stomach and grimaced.

"Easy, Downton. You should be thanking me. The auction is only a week away. Just think this time next week you could be going on a date with your dream girl."

"I don't want a dream girl."

"Oh you will. All men want the perfect woman. Until they get her." She narrowed her eyes on a new mystery he'd just gotten in. She picked up the title and carefully turned the pages.

85

"You didn't ask me what Missy wanted when she came by."

She could feel his eyes on her but managed to keep her expression neutral.

"I'm not one to pry."

He groaned. "She told me she's going to win the auction date with me."

Her gut twisted a little. "Told you she had a thing for you." She carefully turned the page in the book.

"I want you to do me a favor." He walked over and grabbed her arm.

She frowned and looked at him. "I don't do favors for men."

"That's not the kind of favor I want. You're the one who got me into this thing. Now you're going to get me out." He narrowed his eyes.

She laughed. "There's nothing I can do now."

The bell over the door jingled. She stepped away from him just as Donna burst in the door.

She glanced at her and then over at Colin.

"Hello, Ms. Donna. Can I help you with something?" He kept his voice bright.

"Colin. Yes, I'm ah…" She blinked several times, as if she were unsure of what to say. "I saw your bio and picture for the auction date."

He frowned. "It doesn't come out in the paper until tomorrow."

"I didn't see it in the paper. I saw it in the windows, and of course on the bulletin board of the library."

"I was just wondering… is it true?"

"Is what true?" he cocked his head.

Gabriela took a few safe steps away from him.

"Well, I had no idea that we really didn't know you. I'm sorry if you felt like we were not very welcoming to you since you've moved here." She bit her lip and looked more than a bit worried and glanced down at the paper in her hand.

Gabriela silently put the book down and eased toward the door.

"Ms. Donna, is that a copy of the bio?"

She nodded.

"May I see it?"

"Yes of course." She held it out and he took it gently.

"Ms. Donna, I have to confess I didn't write that. Someone else did. I'm sure they put stuff into here to spice things up. You and everyone in town has been more than welcoming to me. So please don't worry yourself."

Her expression relaxed a little. "Are you sure?"

"Absolutely." He gave her a smile and took a step toward Gabriela.

"Okay. Well that makes me feel better. I just wanted you to know that we are so glad you are here and part of our town." She squeezed his arm and walked out the front door.

Gabriela tried to catch the door and follow but Colin grabbed her arm.

"Not so fast." He held her tight as he looked down at the paper in his hand and began reading the bio.

"*Colin Bennett is up for auction! Ever wanted your very own Mr. Darcy? Well, ladies, here's your chance. But it's going to cost you!*"

He looked at her and glared and then looked back at the paper.

"*Colin is a transplant from London England who is single and ready to mingle. But only for the right girl. OR should we say, the right price!*"

"You have got to be kidding me, Gabriela."

She cringed. "It's not as entertaining when you're the one reading it."

87

He is twenty-eight years old and with dark brown hair and mesmerizing green eyes that will look straight into your soul. He owns the local bookstore, The English Rose, and is currently working on the best novel in the world. Favorite author is Jane Austin, of course. He prefers tea to coffee. His perfect date is a romantic dinner followed by snuggling up on the couch and binge watching Downton Abby. "

This time when he looked up Gabriela expected steam to come out of his ears.

Instead he continued reading.

"Dislikes are being left out and not being made to feel welcome especially in a small town. He also cannot abide small talk and unnecessary chatter, and of course cats."

"Don't you love him already? Don't worry! By the end of the date, you will"

She snorted. He jerked his eyes at her. She covered her mouth.

"First of all…"

"I have a feeling there's going to be a lot you aren't liking about the bio."

"You guessed correctly." He glared.

She sighed. "Tell me so I can leave." She crossed her arms, ready to hear him out.

"I don't intend on writing the best novel in the world."

"Come on now. You need to set goals for yourself. I mean anyone can write a mediocre novel. You don't want that do you?" She patted his chest.

"Of course not…" He let go of her arm. "Stop trying to change the conversation. You said Jane Austin is my favorite author. That's not true."

"My bad. She's my favorite author. I started to put down William Shakespeare but I didn't think anyone would buy that. Plus by saying you like Jane Austin makes you more approachable. Which means more people will bid on you."

"Moving down the list. Downton Abby."

"What? Don't like it?"

"I've never watched it."

"I think you're lying."

"Why you…"

"Don't stop now, keep going. I've got only five more minutes for you to air your grievances."

"I don't hate cats. I'm just allergic to them." He lifted his chin.

A slight smile crossed her lips. "You didn't disagree with the part about hating small talk and being left out."

"No one likes small talk."

She nodded in agreement. "So is there anything you like?"

"Not really."

"Well it's too late now. The date is Saturday so wear your best outfit."

"My best outfit is a tux."

"Oh my gosh. You *so* need my help. You can't wear a tux. Don't you have some nice slacks and a nice jacket?"

"I have a camel jacket."

She wanted to roll her eyes. 'Camel colored jacket. Don't say Camel jacket. People around here will think you killed a camel for its skin."

"Maybe it did." He snarked.

She grinned. "Nice one, Downton."

"Stop calling me that."

"Fine. Now that I know you haven't seen the show. What can I call you?"

"Colin."

"Fine. You're really no fun."

"Good then hopefully no one will bid on me."

"Oh they will."

"That's what I'm worried about." He looked dejected.

She felt a little sorry for him. "Come on. It's only one

night. It's not forever. All you have to do is get through one night."

"Promise?"

"Yes."

"Then I want you to do me a favor." He stared at her hard.

"Fine."

"Promise me."

"Fine. I promise." She nodded. She had to hurry or she was going to be walking home.

"I want you to bid on me. And I want you to win."

CHAPTER 18

Colin watched Gabriela's face go from amused to stunned.

He'd caught her off guard. He liked the feeling. Since he met her she constantly caught him off guard. It was nice to return the feeling.

"What?"

"You bid on me and win the date." He crossed his arms across his chest.

"Colin, there's no way..." Her eyes caught movement at the window. Travis was walking across the street and headed for the bookstore.

"I don't want to see him." Her face went pale. "I need to hide."

A smirked settled on his lips. "I've got a secret hiding spot behind the counter. It's behind the wall."

She ran around the counter and pressed the wall. "Where?"

He looked out the window. Travis was almost to the bookstore.

"Colin, where?" She pleaded.

"Not until you agree to win the auction date."

"Colin! I don't have that kind of money! Tell me where the hiding spot it." She feverishly pressed at the wall trying to make it open.

"I'll give you the money. Just bid and win." He smiled.

She groaned. "Fine. I'll bid on you."

"And win. You have to promise me to win the auction."

"Ugh!! Fine. I'll be the winning bid."

He smiled. "Turn the sconce on the wall. A secret panel opens up."

She grabbed the sconce and turned. Just like he said, the wall slid back revealing just enough space for someone to stand.

She stepped inside an the all slid into place.

Travis walked into the bookstore and met Colin's eyes. "I know Gabriela is here. I saw Donna and she said she was here."

"She just left."

"Not out the front door she didn't. He narrowed his eyes at him, clearly not believing him.

"She went out the back.' Colin walked over to the bookshelf and began rearranging some books.

"Then you don't mind if I have a look around." He didn't wait for a reply but began walking down the aisles looking for Gabriela. When he reached the back of the store, he pushed the back door leading to the open.

"Travis I know I'm new here but you can't keep snooping around the back of my shop. That's my personal space and no one is allowed." Colin faced him.

"Not even Gabriela?" Travis crossed his arms.

"That is none of your business. Now you've had your look around and you know she's not here. I think it's time you leave."

Travis glared but relented He walked to the front of the store.

"Travis if you want to talk to her so bad then go to her Aunt's house." Colin leaned against the counter.

"I'd rather not. I'd rather talk to her privately. And I don't want her Aunt butting in." He reached for the door handle and looked over his shoulder. "You tell Gabriela I need to talk to her."

Colin stared back, unspeaking until Travis was out of sight from the shop.

He reached for the sconce and turned. The wall slid away revealing a scared looking Gabriela.

"Are you okay?" He touched her arm.

She slowly nodded. "I'm fine. Thanks for not giving me away." Gone was her fear replaced by the veneer of confidence.

"No problem. Just remember you owe me." He stepped back and let her walk past him.

"Yeah I know." She reached for the door handle just as her aunt pulled up in the truck. "Why do I feel like I just made a deal with the devil?"

"Not sure. Maybe it's because I have mesmerizing green eyes. " He threw her own words back at her and waited for a response. He was disappointed.

Without a word, she walked out of the bookstore. She didn't bother looking back as her aunt pulled onto the street.

He picked up the bio and re-read what she had written. He could just picture the little minx grinning as her fingers flew over the keyboard.

He should have known better. She did ask him questions about what he liked and didn't like. But as usual he didn't volunteer any information.

He looked at the picture she'd taken of him that day behind the church. He never liked having his photo taken.

Unlike his brother who relished in being the center of attention.

She'd done a good job capturing his likeness. Though he wasn't smiling, he seemed amused. Probably at something she'd said.

She was unlike any woman he'd ever met. She was beautiful for sure, but she was so much more.

Quick witted and confident and smart. Things he admired in a woman. Behind the veneer of confidence he saw a vulnerability that he bet very few people saw.

She didn't flaunt her effortless beauty like women he knew. But she didn't seem to hide it either.

She was focused when she had a task at hand, and her idea of the subscription box was brilliant. She had a head for business and marketing, something he could use some help with.

His stomach tightened as he thought about the night of the auction.

What if she changed her mind?

What if she didn't show?

What if she backed out?

Even as these thoughts popped into her head, something inside of him told him, that Gabriela Jackson was not the type to back out of a deal.

Come Saturday night, She'd show up.

And she'd win the date with him.

CHAPTER 19

The week ahead passed painfully slow. Gabriela had tried to stay busy with work around Aunt Agnes's farm but as soon as one chore was done she would quickly find another. She thought throwing herself into work would take her mind off Saturday night. She stood from hoeing a row of string beans and arched her back. Not only was her mind weary, her body hurt.

Every time she thought about the auction date, her stomach would hurt.

She didn't know if she were more worried about what the people of Harland Creek would think about her winning the date or being alone with Colin.

She sighed and assessed her work. All the weeds had been cut away.

"You did good. Although I'm not sure why you are trying to get on my good side."

"You don't have a good side." Gabriela looked at her aunt. "I don't know why you don't just buy canned beans. They're cheap and you don't have to do all this work."

95

"Canned beans don't taste as good as fresh. You know that Gabriela." Aunt Agnes shook her head.

"Did you think any more about the subscription box idea?" She studied her aunt as she gathered some tomatoes off a nearby vine.

She didn't stop her work but shrugged. "I don't think that's for me. I make enough money off my honey to pay the bills. Besides I don't know anything about online sales. I don't even have a computer. And I'm too old to be trying to learn how to use one."

"So you're okay with just getting by." Gabriela narrowed her eyes.

"I'm okay with the way things are. Nothing more nothing less." She stopped gathering tomatoes and put them in her basket. She hooked the wicker basket on her arm and nodded toward the house. "I'm going in to start some dinner. Go wash up. Dinner will be ready in half an hour."

Gabriela curled her fingers into fists, beyond irritated.

Aunt Agnes was the most infuriating woman she knew. Anyone else would jump at the chance to increase their income but not her.

She'd seen the overdue hospital bill that had arrived in the mail. Her aunt had apparently been in the hospital last winter with pneumonia and hadn't bothered telling any of her family.

When she asked her about the bill that morning, Aunt Agnes said she was paying it off little by little and refused to continue talking about it.

If the subscription boxes brought in the kind of money Gabriela had figured when she worked out the business model, then Aunt Agnes would have enough money to pay off her bill within a couple of months.

Sighing she went to the shed and put the work gloves and hoe back where she found them and made her way back to the house. She started to go to the bathroom and shower but instead she headed for the kitchen.

Agnes was putting her cast iron skillet on the stove and getting the ingredients for cornbread together.

"I'll set everything up for the subscription box. I can build out a basic website, set up the ordering and shipping. I'll even help you find a student at school to come over on weekends to help fill the boxes and take orders. You really wouldn't have to lift a finger." Gabriela offered.

"I said no, Gabriela."

"Because it would help you earn some money. Some money you need to help with your hospital bill?" She stared at her incredulous.

Agnes spun around and glared. "I don't want you to help me because then the whole town would be thinking I'm just like you. Trying to make a name for myself and thinking I'm too good for everyone. They'd end up treating me just like you."

Gabriela felt the nausea climb up her throat. She felt like she'd been sucker punched. She and her aunt were never close, but she knew deep down she always had a place to stay.

Now she felt like Agnes was showing her true colors for the first time in her life.

Gabriela stumbled backward and bumped into the frame of the door.

Regret settled into the old woman's face. "Gabriela, I didn't mean that…"

"It's okay. You've made your feelings clear. I won't bring it up again." She ran upstairs into her room.

About thirty minutes later, she heard the knocking on her bedroom door. "I'm not hungry." She pulled the pillow over her head and sunk into covers. She desperately needed a shower but she didn't want to leave the room and have to talk to her aunt.

Finally Aunt Agnes gave up and headed downstairs. Throwing the pillow off the bed, she flung herself on her back and stared up at the ceiling.

She'd never do enough to be forgiven.

She'd always have her past hanging over her head. No matter what had happened that night, the whole town blamed her.

She sat up with anger rushing through her veins.

She couldn't stay here any longer. But she was still low on funds. Biting her lip she thought through her alternatives of how to earn enough money.

Maybe she didn't need money. She could just search for places like RV parks that were always looking for people to work in exchange for a place to stay.

What she needed was a computer.

She glanced at the time on her phone. The library was closed. The only person she knew that lived out here with a computer was the one she'd tried to avoid for the week.

She sat up and headed for the shower. If she were going to ask Colin Bennet for a favor then she needed to look her best.

CHAPTER 20

Colin shoved through the clothes in his closet, rejecting each shirt he picked up.

"I have nothing fashionable, Ringo." He looked at his dog.

Ringo cocked his head and then rested his snout on his front paws in sympathy.

"I'm not an intruder so don't shoot me." Gabriela called out from the living room

He glared at Ringo. "You didn't even bark. Some watch dog you are." He frowned. "I'm in my bedroom. Come on back."

"I make it a point never to go into a man's bedroom without a chaperon or a wedding ring on my finger." She called back.

He snorted and shook his head. "I'm trying to find something to wear for tomorrow."

"Oh, in that case…" Her voice brightened and he heard her light footsteps coming down the hall.

She stepped inside and smiled. "When it comes to fashion, I'm an expert."

He swallowed. "That's what I hear." His heart did a little

flutter. The room seemed to have shrunk and he wondered if the air conditioning had gone out.

"Let's see what you have." She stepped up to the closet and rifled through the clothes. She paused at his tweed jacket. "Wow, this is expensive."

"How do you know that?"

"I'm an expert. I bet I can tell you exactly where in London you bought that very expensive jacket." She waggled her eyebrows.

"I'm sure you can. But it's summer in the South and I'm not wearing a jacket." He took the jacket out of her hand and hung it back up. "I need something more suitable for summer."

"Okay, let's see." She cocked her head and pulled out some white slacks and a chambray shirt.

"That shirt fits a little snug."

"Good. You need to show what people are getting for their money. Besides you are in good shape. Might as well show it off before you get the dad bod."

He ran his hand down his chest. "I'm twenty years away from getting a dad bod. Besides it doesn't matter what I wear, you're the one winning that auction"

"You still have to look nice, Colin' She sighed.

The way she said his name made his chest ache.

She looked over at him. "You okay? You look kind of pale."

"I'm fine. Just some indigestion." He lied and rubbed his chest.

"Here put these on." She handed him the clothes. "And wear those leather shoes I spotted in the closet. I'll be outside. Do you mind if I use your computer? I need to look something up."

"Go ahead. It's on the kitchen table"

"Thanks." She close the bedroom door behind her and Ringo who followed her out.

He quickly changed clothes and glanced at his reflection in the mirror.

He ran his fingers through his hair before walking out into the living room

Gabriela was sitting cross legged on the floor in front of the fireplace. She exited the website she was on when he walked out and looked at Ringo. The dog stared at her adoringly.

"Who's a good boy?" She cooed.

"Me?" Colin held his hands out at his sides.

She laughed and turned to him. When she met his eyes she sobered.

He frowned. 'Don't like it?"

"No, it suits you." She nodded and her eyes darted to his shoes. "And I'm impressed you didn't put socks with those shoes. Every man in town would have worn white socks."

"I see you've gotten Ringo to fall in love with you. It usually takes him time to get used to someone."

"I'm not special. I bet he's like that with all the ladies." She gave him a kiss on the nose.

"Actually he growled at Missy."

She barked out a laugh and rubbed his head. "You *are* a good boy!"

He held out a hand and helped her to her feet. She stood and frowned. "If you want to sell the package, you need to unbutton that top button."

He unbuttoned one button and tried to see his reflection in the living room mirror.

She turned up his collar and then ruffled his hair a bit. "See, that looks better. Not that you need any help." She bit her lip and glanced away, distracted.

"Forgive my manners. Would you like some tea or something to drink?" He headed into the kitchen.

"Tea sounds good. And if you have a scone lying around throw that on the saucer.

He grinned as he put the electric kettle on. Her wit always amused him.

She walked into the kitchen and sat at the island. Her gaze landed on the box he'd received from England. "What's that? The return address says England. Something from your family?"

"Something." He pulled down two tea cups and placed them on the counter. "You asked me why I moved away from England. Well it has a lot to do with my family."

"I can relate to that." She deadpanned.

"And it's something I've never told anyone." He turned and looked at her.

"You don't have to tell me if you don't want to. It's your business. I didn't mean to pry the other night."

"It might be good for me to confide in someone." He admitted. He poured the hot water over the tea bags dangling in the cups. He placed one in front of her and then set his down on the counter. He walked over to the box and picked it up. He carried it over to the island and set it down.

"I grew up in a wealthy family. My parents, grandparent and brother all lived rather close to each other in London. And we have a family estate in the countryside."

"Sounds ideal." She took her tea bag out and placed it on the tea bag holder he slid over to her.

"You would think so. My family is very old school. They value tradition and making sure the next generation is on top of the world."

She said nothing but listened intently.

"My parents expected me to go to law school. My father was a lawyer and his father before him. It's kind of tradition."

"And you didn't want to follow tradition?"

"I tried to follow their plans for my life. I actually attended Oxford a few semesters. I even met someone there. Her name was Margaret and she'd gotten a scholarship and was completely opposite of me. She had worked hard at everything in life and wanted something better.

"Did you two fall in love?"

"Yes. And she encouraged me to follow my heart and tell my parents I wanted to major in English."

"So I took her home with me on Christmas break. She charmed my parents and my brother. And I felt sure that would work in my favor when I approached them about changing my major." He took a sip of his tea.

"What happened?"

"Before Christmas Eve dinner, I gathered my parents together and told them my plans. My mother looked at me like I had lost my mind and my father went into a rage. He forbid it and he threatened to cut me out of the will and disinherit me."

"Wow." She gave him a sympathetic look.

"Anyway, I was emboldened by Margaret and told them I didn't need their money. I had some of my own from an inheritance from one of my uncles. So I stormed out of the room to find Margaret. I was going to gather our things and leave. I figured we could catch a flight to Paris and spend Christmas there."

"Sounds romantic."

"Except when I found Margaret she was kissing my brother under the mistletoe."

Her mouth dropped open.

"I hit Charles and told Margaret we were leaving. She told me I was being irrational and that it was just an innocent kiss. When I told her that my parents were disinheriting me, her demeanor changed. She went pale. My parents burst into the room at the commotion and told me to leave. I did. Margaret decided to stay."

"Sounds like she wanted to be with you because she found out you were rich."

"You would be right." He took a sip of tea.

"And what happened to her?"

He gave a wry smile and opened the box. "Well she's in England and she married Charles." He pulled out the note from his brother announcing the birth.

Gabriela covered her mouth as she read the birth announcement. "Oh Colin. So they got married?"

"Yes. Soon after that Christmas. I left England and invested some of my inheritance in the Bookstore and am taking some English classes on line. In the meantime, I'm writing my book." He shoved his hand through his hair. "I guess time will tell if I made the worst decision of my life."

"Or the best decision." She covered his hand with hers. "I'm sorry that happened to you."

His heart beat a little faster. "I've never told anyone that before."

"I'm glad you told me." Her eyes were sad.

"Well it's the least I can do since you will be bidding on me for this date."

She moved her hand away. "About that."

"You cannot renege on the deal."

"What if the price goes up? Like really high? I mean Missy hasn't had a date in a while. And you being such a catch, I'm sure she's going to max out a brand new credit card."

"No matter what, you have to win the bid."

"Colin.."

He walked around the counter and spun her around in the chair until she was looking at him. He placed his hands on either side of her face. "Gabriela. I'm serious. You promised me. You promised you would be the winning bidder."

She grabbed his hand. 'What if the bid goes up to one thousand dollars?"

"Then bid it." He narrowed his eyes.

"What if it's up to four thousand dollars?" She looked grieved.

"Then bid it. I'm serious Gabriela. Don't you dare let anyone else win me. Promise me now." He held her gaze to his.

Something shifted in her expression. A vulnerable softness entered her eyes. Slowly she nodded. "Okay I'll be the winning bidder."

He smiled and pressed his forehead to hers. "Thank God. I thought for a second you were going to let Missy beat you."

She laughed and he lifted his head. He had an overwhelming urge to kiss her. But he saw the hesitancy in her eyes and knew he'd stepped across the line.

He let go of her and stepped back. Ringo saw his opportunity and wedged his way in between them. He rested his snout on her leg and whined.

"Did you find what you were looking for on the computer?"

"Not really. "She laughed and rubbed Ringo's head. "I guess I need to be going."

"Are you sure? I'm making lamb chops tonight.'

"Hmmm. Tempting but no. I have to get going. Tomorrow is going to be busy and I have to decide what to wear if I'm bidding on you. I'm thinking a short red dress and high heels. To give the town something to talk about."

"You don't need to do that. You can show up in a garbage bag and have half the men after you." He laughed.

She snorted. "I'll split the difference. And see what I come up with."

CHAPTER 21

She'd never been afraid of crowds until she was standing in the Harland Creek community center. She'd arrived after her aunt and tried to make her way through the crowd without drawing attention. She noticed that Stacey and Missy both were wearing what looked like cocktail attire and trying way too hard. Despite how they had treated her she felt a little bad for them.

She headed for a corner in the room and looked at the paddle she'd gotten when she registered to bid. Number 13. She sighed when she'd been given the number.

She glanced around the room and spotted Tabitha Miller. She met Gabriela's gaze and brightened. She headed in her direction.

"Hey Gabriela. Glad to see you are here. I see you're planning on bidding for the date." Tabitha grinned and held up her own paddle.

"How bad do you want to win?" Gabriela cringed.

"Not bad enough to go over my limit. Which is one hundred dollars. I figure I'll be out early." Tabitha shrugged, obviously unconcerned.

"Oh." She relaxed a little. "I guess you're surprised so see me here."

"No. Everyone showed up." Tabitha looked across the room. "Wow. Look at Colin. He certainly dressed to impress."

Gabriela jerked her head in the direction of where Tabitha was staring. Colin had been greeted by Pastor John who was vigorously shaking his hand. He was dressed in the outfit she'd picked out for him, right down to the loafers. He stepped away from the Pastor and looked around, running his hand through his hair.

When their eyes met, he smiled.

And her heart lurched.

"Earth to Gabriela." Tabitha said.

She tore her gaze away and looked at her. "Yes?"

"You didn't hear a word I said." Tabitha narrowed her eyes and then looked over at Colin. "Hmmmm. Now I see."

"You see what?" She lifted her chin. "What were you saying earlier?"

"It's not important." She grinned. "Where are you sitting?"

"I'll probably stand here."

"Perfect then I'll stand here too." Tabitha giggled. "I have a feeling this is going to be a good show."

"What's gotten into you?" Gabriela glared.

"From the look Colin was giving you, I'm guessing he's hoping you are going to win the date."

"Why don't you go bid on some of the silent auction items?" Gabriela suggested. "I'm sure there's something that might capture your interest."

"Oh I'm already captivated." Tabitha grinned.

Gabriela glared.

"Fine. I'm going, I'm going." Tabitha laughed and headed over to the tables lined with silent auction items.

Gabriela was busy watching Tabitha that she didn't notice Colin walkup behind her."

JODI ALLEN BRICE

"Hey."

She jumped and spun around. "What are you doing?" She felt her face flame and she took a step away.

"Just saying hello. Thanks for holding up your end of the bargain."

"I said I'd do it, didn't I?" She fanned herself with the paddle.

He picked up her auction paddle. "Ah lucky number thirteen."

She snatched it out his hand. "More like unlucky. Look, you can't be standing by me. Go mingle with the others."

"I don't feel like mingling." He glanced down at her outfit. "You look pretty."

"I thought about wearing a red dress with a large A plastered across the top." She touched the collar of her white blouse and glanced down at her black pencil skirt.

He laughed. "I'm glad you went in this direction."

She shifted her weigh in her high heel black shoes. "You may not by the time this night is over."

"Gabriela." He touched her elbow.

She pulled back like she'd been touched by fire. "Stop doing that."

"Doing what?" He looked confused.

"Touching me. Talking to me. People are going to talk." She glanced around hoping no one was watching their interaction.

Missy was glaring at her from across the room.

"People are going to talk no matter what. You shouldn't worry about it." He leaned in and whispered.

She went wide eyed. "Are you wearing cologne?"

"Yeah. Do you not like it?" He cocked his head. 'Are you feeling okay? You look a little flushed."

She liked it alright. She liked it too much.

"I'll be back." She hurried out of the door leading to the

nearest exit. Stepping outside she inhaled the humid night air.

She felt lightheaded and nauseated.

This whole thing was a mistake.

She never should have agreed to bid on Colin. She wished she could just get in a car and drive somewhere far away where no one knew her. She'd even settle for a cabin on a mountain, far from humanity.

"What are you doing out here?" Agnes walked out the door and stared at her.

"It's just really crowded in there. Just needed some air."

"Humph." Aunt Agnes crossed her arms over her chest. "Did you see half of the women all dressed up like they are going to a ball?"

"Not really." She lied. She didn't want to talk about this with Aunt Agnes. She just wanted to be alone.

"It looks like everyone is bidding on the silent auction items. We only have another hour before the bid closes and winners are announced. "

She closed her eyes and nodded. "Okay. I'll come back inside in a minute." She looked at her aunt.

"You okay?" Aunt Agnes looked at her with concern in her eyes.

"Yeah." She lied.

Aunt Agnes didn't look like she believed her, but finally moved to walk back inside the community center. She cast one last look over her shoulder before walking inside.

CHAPTER 22

Colin's stomach turned. He searched the crowd for Gabriela but couldn't find her. After she'd gone outside, he had not seen her come back.

Every single woman in Harland Creek and surrounding towns came up to him to chat. Most were fascinated that he was from England. Some were fascinated that he was a writer. But all were fascinated that he was single guy looking for a girl.

"I can't believe we have so much in common." A woman named Chloe purred at his side. She looked to be around twenty and much too young for him. "My favorite show is Downton Abby. I read you love that show."

"Actually…." His words trailed off when his gaze landed on Gabriela standing in the sea of people. She always stood out.

"If you'll excuse me. I think the charity committee needs to see me." He made a bee line for Gabriela.

Just before he reached her Missy stepped in his path. "Hello Colin." She batted her eyes.

"Missy, if you'll excuse me…"

She wrapped her hand on his arm and looked up long-ingly. "I just want you to know that I think it's wonderful that you are doing this for charity. Not many men would sacrifice themselves for such a noble cause."

"It's not that much of a sacrifice. Just dinner." He frowned.

"And I want you to know I intend on being the highest bidder." She smiled slowly.

"There are a lot of bidders. You don't know that someone will outbid you." He gave her a sympathetic smile. He didn't want to give her any kind of hope.

"If they take credit card then I'll be the highest bidder." She assured her.

His hackles went up. He didn't care for how she was looking at him or what she was saying.

"If you'll excuse me."

He walked around Missy and headed towards Gabriela. She saw he was intent on walking over and went wide-eyed.

He blocked her before she could get away. "Hey, is every-thing okay?"

"Just fine and dandy." She looked away.

"Doesn't sound like it. You're not backing out are you?"

"No." She met his eyes and lifted her chin. "A deal's a deal."

He breathed out a sigh of relief. "Good." He glanced over his shoulder. "Missy is making me very uncomfortable."

"I'm sure she'll leave you alone after tonight." Gabriela assured.

"I hope so." He glanced at the time on his watch. "Give me your banking information so I can transfer the money once the bidding is over."

She wrote down her info and handed it to him.

"I guess it's almost time. I need to get back up front." He made his fingers into fists.

She nodded and took a drink from a bottled water.

He felt the need to say more but couldn't find the exact words. This wasn't like him. He always knew what to say.

Shaking his head, he blamed it on a bad case of nerves.

He gave her arm a squeeze and then headed back to the front of the room.

CHAPTER 23

"*A*ll the silent auction items have now been picked up. If you want to see if you won an item you bid on, then please see Donna at the entrance. " Elizabeth Harland clapped her hands together. "Now for the event everyone is waiting for, let's get to our auction date."

Everyone sent up cheers. Everyone except Gabriela.

Her stomach twisted in a knot.

Tabitha sidled up to her in the back of the room and sat on the vacant seat next to her.

"How much do you think the winning bid will be?" Tabitha leaned over

"No idea. Probably some ridiculous amount." Gabriela blinked rapidly. She wiped her sweaty palms on her thighs.

"Maybe we should move up front, you know, get better seats." Tabitha offered

"No. This is perfect."

"If anyone needs a bidding paddle you have about a minute to get one." Elizabeth gave a warning.

"I wonder if this is going to be a yearly event?" Tabitha asked.

"What are you talking about?" She was getting irritated at Tabitha's mundane chit chat. She was about thirty seconds from a full blown anxiety attack. Couldn't Tabitha see that?

"Do you think they'll have an auction date every year?"

"Probably not. Everyone will be very disappointed in this year's event and then they'll forbid it from ever happening again." Gabriela blurted out the words and then froze

Tabitha blinked but said nothing.

"And now please help me welcome our date of the evening, Colin Bennett." Elizabeth announced.

Everyone clapped and more than a few women whistled.

Gabriela felt her face change colors. From pale to red. She wasn't sure if she was going to faint or throw up.

"Colin hales from London England...." The words grew into white noise in Gabriela's ears. Tiny purple stars began to swim in front of her eyes.

Before she knew it, paddles were going up around the room. The white noise grew louder between her ears and she couldn't make out what the bid was up to. She pressed her hand to her stomach but couldn't bring herself to raise her own bidding paddle.

"Oh my gosh. I can't believe the bidding has gone that high." Tabitha muttered.

Gabriela blinked.

"Looks like Missy is going to win." Tabitha looked at her with a seriousness she didn't normally wear. "If you want him, you better fight for him."

She looked at the front of the room. Her gaze met Colin's worried gaze. No wonder. He was beginning to wonder if she were going to keep up her end of the bargain.

"Going once.....going twice.."

Forcing her muscles to cooperate, Gabriela raised her paddle in the air.

A gasp went up around the room.

"Number 13 has the five thousand dollar bid. Do I hear six thousand?"

Missy narrowed her gaze on her. She jumped up from her seat and threw her paddle down. "She can't bid. It's not fair."

All eyes were on her.

She was pretty sure she was going to throw up.

"Everyone has a chance to bid, Missy. " Elizabeth spoke in a calm voice. "Now if you would like to make a higher bid you can."

Gabriela swallowed and looked at Colin. In his expression he was trying to encourage her to stay the course and win the auction.

The white noise between her ears slowly died down and was replaced by the growing thud of her heartbeat.

"The bid is five thousand dollars; do I hear six thousand?" Elizabeth asked.

When no one else raised their paddles, Elizabeth slammed down the gavel. "Sold! Gabriela Jackson has won the date with Colin Bennett." She announced.

Slight applause went around the room.

Tabitha whistled and congratulated her on winning the auction.

Aunt Agnes shot daggers at her from across the room.

People started getting up and moving about.

She started to tremble as Colin walked over to her.

"What have I done?" She muttered to herself.

"You kept your promise." Colin took her hand in his.

CHAPTER 24

"*D*on't forget to pay before you leave." Elizabeth reminded Gabriela.

Gabriela's eyes grew wide.

Colin squeezed her hand. "Don't worry. I just transferred the money into your account."

She looked like she didn't believe him and pulled out her phone. After a quick keystrokes she froze and looked up at him with unbelief.

"You think I would have gone to all this trouble and not given you the money?"

"I don't know what I believe?" Her shoulders sank. "I need to get this paid before they start a rumor about me not paying my bills." She walked over to Donna who looked at her in surprise.

"Colin. I'm sorry I couldn't save you." Missy eased over to him. "I did my best to win the auction but I let you down."

He rubbed his hand across the back of his neck. "You know Missy. I think I'm going to have a great time on my date with Gabriela. She's smart, she's witty and she doesn't go around putting other people down."

Missy reared back in shock. She quickly composed herself. "She's got you fooled too, I see. Enjoy your date.' She stormed away.

He kept his gaze on Gabriela and saw how the crowd seemed to part as she walked.

Harland Creek had been nothing but welcoming and warm. He wanted to take the microphone and tell everyone to remember what their Bible said and how they acted in church should mirror how they lived every day.

Gabriela walked back over to him. "The money went through. I hope you appreciate the bullet I took for you. I didn't think the town could hate me anymore. I was totally wrong." She sighed and stuck her phone in her purse.

He frowned. "I hate the way they are acting to you. I'll make it up to you on our date."

"Date?" She jerked her head towards him.

Her words stung. "Well yeah. The dinner is tomorrow night. I already got confirmation from the restaurant. And Grayson said he is doing something special with the zip line."

"Oh, I mean I didn't actually think you wanted to take me on a date." She glanced around the room. "But I guess we have to make an effort to keep up appearances."

"Oh Colin. Oh. Gabriela." Wilma tired's voice had them both turning.Wilma's daughter pushed the wheelchair up to them. She tightened the white shawl around her shoulders. Her shoulders slumped slighted under the soft green pant suit she was wearing. She wore a pink turban to hide her recent hair loss and her pale skin. Though she was tired, she wore a smile.

She reached out for both of their hands. They smiled and held the woman's hand.

"I just can't thank you enough for doing this. Colin, how very selfless of you to volunteer to be auctioned off." She pressed his hand to her cheek. "You'll never know how much it means."

"You're very welcome. Anything for you, Wilma." He covered her hand with his.

"And Gabriela. You are such a generous woman to bid so high. I thought for sure that Missy was going to win." She motioned with her finger for her to bend down. Gabriela leaned closer.

"I'm glad you beat her. I'm not sure I trust someone who parks in the handicap spot at the library."

Gabriela grinned.

"I'll let you two talk. I'm pretty tired. All this excitement has worn me out. I just wanted to come over and thank you both." She gave them a wave as her daughter pushed the wheelchair toward the door.

"That was nice of her." Gabriela cocked her head

"That's what I like about Harland Creek. The hometown people are so welcoming and kind."

Gabriela snorted.

He inwardly cringed. He forgot her perspective of the town was skewed.

"I'll pick you up tomorrow at ten."

"In the morning?" She grimaced.

"Yes. So no late night walks tonight." He deadpanned.

She rolled her eyes and hoisted her purse on her shoulder. "I can't promise anything." She gave him one last look as she walked out the door.

CHAPTER 25

*A*unt Agnes continued to give Gabriela the cold shoulder for the next twenty four hours. When she greeted her aunt to get some coffee, Aunt Agnes ignored her. Whenever she would walk into a room, Aunt Agnes would walk out. She answered the phone when it rang, she handed it to her aunt. Aunt Agnes didn't say a word but hung up the phone.

It was official.

Her aunt was completely icing her out.

She barely heard the knock on the door because she was so lost in her thoughts.

Realizing her aunt wasn't going to get the door, she sighed stomped toward the incessant knocking.

Without looking she threw open the door.

"You look very excited for our date." Colin arched his brow.

"Sorry. The atmosphere has been kind of icy around here this morning." She looked at his outfit of jeans and a T-shirt and glanced at her cut off denim and shirt. "I haven't had time to change."

"Don't" He grabbed her hand. "What you are wearing is perfect. I'll bring you back here so you can change for dinner."

She didn't resist but followed him out to his car. He opened the passenger's door and held it open for her.

"You don't have to do that."

"I know. I want to." He waited until she was buckled in before shutting the door.

She glanced back at the house as they pulled away.

"Aunt Agnes is glaring at me."

"You're too far away to tell if she's glaring at you."

"Fine. She's very upset because she has her arms crossed over her chest and her chin is lifted up. And if it were humanly possible, smoke would be coming out of her ears and circling that ridiculous bee hat she wears all the time."

Colin laughed. "That's very descriptive."

"Thanks. You can use it in a book."

"I might do that." He turned his car toward the direction of the McCade Farm. "Grayson already called me this morning and told me he would be ready for us.'

"So we really are ziplining? She looked over at him.

"Yes. I hope you're not disappointed."

"No. I don't think I've ever been ziplining."

'Well it's not like ziplining through the jungle but it should be fun.'

"Fun. That's not something I've thought about in a while.' The words spilled out.

"What do you think about?"

"Surviving. Making a career for myself. Something other than modeling."

"Marketing?"

"Yes, actually. It's like when I get an idea in my head I keep working on it, finding different ways to market it best."

He listened as she talked, glad she was so comfortable talking with him.

He turned into the driveway that would lead them up to Grayson's house. He'd only been out once before when Grayson had thrown a BBQ. He'd invited the whole town. Trying to get to meet the townspeople, Colin had come and brought some English Scones which were a big hit.

He parked and killed the engine. Grayson waved and stepped off his front porch.

They both got out of the car.

Gabriela's stomach twisted a little. She knew Grayson wasn't her biggest fan.

"Gabriela!" Heather Smith appeared from behind the barn with Petunia in tow. Petunia was a goat and a gift from Grayson when they started dating. Everywhere Heather went Petunia went as well. Sometimes that proved difficult because Heather lived and worked on Elizabeth Harland's flower farm and the goat tended to eat up the flowers

Heather ran over and gave her a hug. Gabriela saw the way Grayson was watching their interaction and quickly pulled back.

"Hi Heather." She bent and patted Petunia between the ears. "She's getting really big. I can remember when she was little."

"I know." Heather smiled "It's getting harder to keep her at the flower farm so I keep her here at Grayson's barn overnight. "I miss her terribly at night. But I know if she needs something then Grayson will take care of her.

"Well maybe one day you two will be under the same roof." Gabriela arched her brow.

Grayson and Colin walked up to them. "Whenever I broach the subject of marriage, she tells me she doesn't want to rush into anything." Grayson put his arm around her shoulders.

She leaned into him. "I just enjoying finally making a home for myself here in Harland Creek. There will be plenty of time for….long term plans."

"She can't even say the words." Grayson shook his head.

Everyone laughed.

"I didn't ask when we talked but I hope we are dressed properly for ziplining." Colin glanced toward the woods where the zipline was.

"You're both fine." Grayson assured.

"Have you ziplined before?" Heather asked

"I haven't." Gabriela answered.

"I have. A few times in Puerto Rico." Colin shrugged. "I was actually surprised to hear you had one set up out here on the farm.

"Well don't get all excited." Grayson clapped him on the shoulder. "It's nothing extravagant."

"I'm sure it will be fun, none the less." Gabriela offered.

"We'll take the side by side down." Grayson pointed to the all-terrain vehicle.

Grayson and Heather and Petunia got into the front seat while Gabriela and Colin climbed into the back.

Grayson started the engine and they took off down a small dirt road no bigger than a deer trail.

After traveling a small distance in the woods they came to a clearing. A small creek separated Grayson's land from Elizabeth's land. A large oak tree on Grayson's property had a wood ladder leading up to a deck with the zipline. The zipline ended on Elizabeth's property with a large oak tree and an enclosed wood platform. That platform had tiny twinkle lights hanging round the side.

"Wow, I bet that's pretty at night." Gabriela said looking up.

"It is. Just wait until you get to the other side." Heather winked.

"All you have to do is climb up and grab the handle and step off. Once you get to the other side, you can pull it back by this lever. Go back over the small bridge below to get back to this platform to keep ziplining. There' s no safety harness because it goes over the creek and well it's not that high up. I suppose I should have thought about putting one in." Grayson scratched the back of his neck

"I'm sure it will be fine. Looks like the creek is up a bit."

"Yeah, it's pretty deep. It's deep enough if you want to let go and drop in the water." Heather smiled.

"Do you do that?" Gabriela grinned.

"Sometimes." Heather shrugged. "Did you wear your swim suit under your clothes?"

"No. I didn't know that was an option. I'll remember next time."

"So we are going to leave and let you guys have at it. You can go back and forth the zip line as many times as you want. " Grayson held his hand out for Heather and they waved goodbye.

"Ready?" Colin eyed her.

"Sure. You want to go first?" She bit her lip.

"I can, if you're scared?"

"I didn't say I was scared." She lifted her chin and stepped up to the ladder. Slowly she began to climb. When she got to the top she looked down.

Colin climbed up behind her.

"It's higher than it looks." She said peering over the edge.

"You can always let go over the water if you want." He took her hand.

Her heart quickened. His words were heavy with meaning.

"Ready?"

"Now or never." She took the handle and stepped to the edge. Holding on tight she stepped out onto air.

She flew through the air, the wind blowing her hair. Small dappled patches of sunlight cut through leaves and landed on her face as she laughed. When she reached the other side she stepped onto the platform and turned around.

"That was wonderful." She called out to Colin.

"Good! I'm pulling it back so I can go."

She nodded and turned around to examine the view from her perch. She walked to the edge and noticed there were two large pillows and a blanket spread out on the platform. A bouquet of roses sat between the pillows.

She turned just as Colin ziplined toward her. When he reached her he easily stepped on to the platform.

"Did you know they were going to do this?" She pointed to the cozy area of pillows and flowers.

"No, but it's nice. Isn't that Elizabeth's property on this side." He rested his hand on her lower back and pointed.

"It is. We used to come here every Easter for an Easter Egg hunt. Elizabeth always had the best prizes. I found the prize egg when I was eight. She had buried it under the only tall weed in the pasture. It was a five dollar bill. That was a lot of money to an eight year old. Did your family celebrate holidays?"

"We did but yours sounds better."

"How is that?"

"Well our holidays always turned into elaborate parties put on to impress the neighbors. Our Easter Egg hunts involved dressing up in our finest and getting our pictures taken before hunting eggs. It was always a catered event with a lot of food and even more champagne."

"Sounds like a party."

"It was. All the holidays were parties. And not in a fun relaxed way either. More like where children should be seen and not heard."

"That's too bad. You'll find Harland Creek is a very family

friendly town."

"Maybe you'll feel that way yourself again somehow."

"I doubt that." She shrugged. "Look there's a basket too. Let's see what's in it."

She didn't wait but went ahead and sat. The platform was in the shade and the breeze was comfortable.

He sat beside her and opened up the basket. Inside was two champagne glasses, a bottle of apple cider, and a tin of shortbread. There was also a leather bound copy of Pride and Prejudice."

"My favorite book. I didn't expect that." Gabriela smiled.

"I had them add it to the basket. I had a hunch you would like it."

"I do." She ran her fingers over the leather."

Colin took the bottle and poured them both a glass of cider. She opened the tin of shortbread and handed him one.

"I bet Donna made these. She makes the best shortbread. She usually gives them as gifts for Christmas." Gabriela sighed as the cookie melted in her mouth.

"These are good. Just as good as any bakery in England." He nodded.

They sat quietly for a while, eating shortbread and sipping on apple cider, while the breeze caressed their face. He took the book and began reading.

For the first time since coming back to Harland Creek, Gabriela felt at peace. She leaned her head back against the tree and closed her eyes.

"Gabriela?"

She blinked and lifted her head from his shoulder. "Sorry. I guess I fell asleep. Bet that's never happened to you before." She rubbed her eyes.

"It's okay. I didn't want to wake you. You looked so peaceful." He brushed the hair out of her face and looked into her eyes.

She didn't move away but leaned into him. She'd never felt so at home with someone.

She knew the look in his green eyes. He was going to kiss her.

Just then the hum of Grayson's ATV had her looking down.

"Hey guys." Grayson parked and jumped out of the vehicle. "We need to keep you guys on schedule. Your next stop is light lunch at Elizabeth's farm."

"What?" She looked from Grayson to Colin. "I thought the only thing that was scheduled was the ziplining and dinner."

"I think some things got added at the last minute." He rubbed the back of his head. "We should get going." He stood and helped her up.

She climbed down the ladder followed by Colin.

"How did you guys like the zipline?" Grayson asked as they drove back to the farm.

"I can see why Heather likes it so much. It was very kind of you to make it for her." Gabriela called out from the backseat.

"When Petunia was smaller she put her in a baby carrier that straps to the front. And she would go across it with the goat." Grayson laughed.

"I would pay money to see that." Colin laughed.

Grayson pulled up to Colin's car. Everyone got out.

"Thanks for this. It was very nice." Gabriela smiled.

"I'm glad you both enjoyed it." Grayson looked at her.

She could tell he was trying to be polite because Colin was there, not because he meant it.

She shrugged it off and headed for Colin's car. Colin and Grayson shook hands before they climbed back into the car to head for Elizabeth's farm.

CHAPTER 26

Elizabeth waved to them from her porch.

Colin hurried around the car to open Gabriela's door before she could do it herself.

"Hey you two!" Elizabeth called out.

"Hey!" Gabriela smiled wide.

He could tell her demeanor had changed and she greeted Elizabeth more warmly than she had Grayson.

From what he knew of Elizabeth Harland she had always been a woman who tried to stay out of other people's business and treated everyone with kindness.

When Elizabeth reached them she threw her arms around Gabriela and hugged her tight.

"Don't you look pretty?" Elizabeth patted her arms.

"Not really. Colin picked me up before I was ready so all he got was this." She threw her arms out and looked down at her cut off shorts and T-shirt."

"And she still looks lovely." Colin insisted. "Besides, I promised to take her home so she could change for dinner tonight."

"Well, right now I have a nice lunch ready for you both. Follow me out to the barn."

Gabriela gave him an odd look. He wanted to ask questions but he just went along with it.

They went around the farmhouse to the barn. Set under the large oak tree, was a small table and two chairs. The table was covered in a pretty floral tablecloth. The table was set along with a small but beautiful bouquet of pink and white flowers. There was a tower of finger sandwiches, scones, and small cookies. A pot of hot tea sat beside two tea cups.

"It's high tea. This is beautiful." Gabriela gasped.

"Thank you, dear. I knew you have the roses over at Grayson's so I decided on some inpatients and some zinnias along with some Queen Anne's lace to fill it out."

"You did a wonderful job. But you always do, Mrs. Harland." Colin complimented her.

"Thank you, dear. Now both of you sit and eat. Stay as long as you want. I want you to enjoy yourselves." Elizabeth smiled and then ambled back to the house.

"You two seem to get along well." Colin held out her chair.

She looked up at him as she sat. "Ms. Elizabeth has always been nice to me. She and Aunt Agnes are best friends so I saw her a lot when I was growing up."

He sat opposite of her. "So her opinion of you never changed."

"No. She's been a constant in my life when I needed one. I'm lucky she still talks to me." Gabriela gently placed the linen napkin in her lap.

He sat opposite and reached for the napkin. "Well, she's the lucky one."

She chortled and shook her head. "I'll pour the tea." She reached for the teapot and carefully poured tea into his cup before pouring into hers. "Hand me your plate.'

He did and watched as she picked out some sandwiches and cookies and placed them on his plate. He waited until she fixed her own plate.

She took a sip and sighed. 'That' s really good tea."

"It's the tea I sell in my bookstore." He grinned, glad she liked it.

"Maybe you should be doing a tea subscription box."

"There are too many people selling tea. I don't think I could compete."

"True. But it could increase sales at your book store in another way. You should promote your book. Readers are always fascinated by an author who owns a bookstore."

"My book is not finished. Not yet."

"Well when it is you should consider marketing it well." She nibbled on a sandwich.

"When it's done, I'll hire you to do the marketing."

"Really? You'd do that?" Her eyes widened.

"Yes. I need someone who knows what they are doing. Lord knows I don't have a clue when it comes to that. I just want to write." He bit into his sandwich.

"I'll hold you to that." She grinned.

After finishing off the sandwiches and sweet treats, they took a walk among the flowers. He'd never seen Gabriela smile so much. She was relaxed and happy. She didn't even pull away when he reached for her hand.

As they wandered among the flowers he couldn't help but wonder what it would be like to have her at his side in life. Did she even think about ever getting married? Starting a family? Settling down?

He even imagined bringing her home to England to meet his parents. He grinned as he imagined the look of jealousy on his brother's face when he got a look at Gabriela.

"What are you grinning about?" She frowned.

He sobered and shook his head. "Nothing. Just thinking about tonight."

She arched her brow and held up her finger. "Don't get any ideas. I'm not that kind of girl. You might get lucky if you get a kiss."

His eyebrows shot up. "Already promising a kiss at the end of the date."

She scowled. "Never mind. I take it back." She started back the way they came.

"Wait." He laughed and quickly caught up her. "I'm just teasing." He reached for her hand. "I would never expect anything from you. Not even a kiss at the end of a date."

Her expression softened. "You're forgiven. But it's only because of your accent."

"And not my mesmerizing green eyes?" He teased.

"Well maybe." She grinned.

CHAPTER 27

She clasped her hands in her lap and stared straight ahead.

"You look beautiful." Colin said softly.

"You already told me that." She rubbed her hand across the white summer dress she'd chosen to wear. She paired it with some fashionable nude heels and gold hoop earrings and bangle bracelets.

"You seem nervous. You weren't nervous today." He noticed.

"That's because we were by ourselves, not surrounded in a crowded restaurant with half the town looking at me." Her stomach twisted.

"It will be fine." He reached over and squeezed her hand.

She took a deep cleansing breath when he turned on Main Street. When he pulled into the parking spot, she thought about jumping out of the car and running back to Aunt Agnes' house.

"It's just dinner, Gabriela." His voice was soft and reassuring.

"Doesn't feel like it." She blinked and then looked at him.

She shook her head. "Come on. Let's go in." She didn't wait for him to open her door but stepped out.

He held the door of the restaurant for her allowing her to walk in first. She stopped in shocked to see half the town sitting down to dinner.

"Great." She muttered.

"It's fine. Just smile." He whispered near her ear.

She pasted a smile on.

"Maybe by the time we leave your smile will be genuine."

"Don't hold your breath." She said under her breath.

He laughed and followed the hostess to be seated.

Gabriela blinked. "In the middle of the room. They seat us in the middle of the room."

Colin grinned and pulled out her chair. "It will be fine. Just concentrate on what you want to order for dinner. "

She sat and put her napkin on her lap.

"Hello, Colin. So glad to see you here." Eliza Ross gave him a big smile and ignored Gabriela.

Eliza had gone to high school with Gabriela. While they had been in some classes together, they'd never really hung out in the same circles but they'd always been friendly. After the accident Eliza, like the rest of the town had distanced herself.

"Hello Eliza. I didn't know you were working here." Colin smiled politely.

The girl rolled her eyes. "Yes. It's the only job I can find at the moment. Until college starts back. I guess I'll be spending my holiday break waiting tables."

"Well, I might could use some help at the English Rose around Christmas if you are interested in some part time work."

"Really?" Her eyes widened. "That would be wonderful." She hugged the menus to her chest and looked lost in a dream. "To be surrounded by all those wonderful books. It must be heaven."

"Eliza, are you going to stand there daydreaming or are you going to wait on the customers." Maxwell Higgins the owner shook his head as he passed the table.

"Oh, sorry." She shook her head and quickly handed the menus to her and Colin. "What would you like to drink?" She pulled a pen and pad out of the pocket of the short apron she wore.

"Sweet tea, please." Gabriela glanced at the menu.

"The same for me." Colin smiled.

Eliza headed for the kitchen.

She closed her menu and took careful glances at people around the room.

Surprisingly most were studying their plates but a few were casting curious stares in their direction.

Eliza hurried back and set their drinks down in front of them. "Have you decided on what you want for dinner? Or do you need a little more time?"

"I know what I want." Gabriela handed her menu to Eliza. "I'll have the filet with loaded baked potato and Caesar salad."

"I think I'll have to same." Colin handed his menu to Eliza.

"I'll put that right in." She gave them both a smile and headed back to the kitchen.

"You know Eliza?" Colin asked.

We went to school together."

"Really?" He cocked his head.

"You seem surprised." Gabriela took a sip of her tea.

"You seem older than her. More mature."

"That's probably because I've seen more of life than her."

"My grandmother called it being an old soul." Colin nodded.

She grinned. "You're off your game, Colin. Don't ever tell a woman she's old."

He laughed. "Sorry. Haven't had a date in a while. Why don't we talk about something else."

"Like what?"

"For starters, what is your middle name."

She rolled her eyes.

"Come on. You know mine. It's only fair."

"Fine. It's Hope."

"Gabriela Hope. That's beautiful."

"Thanks."

Their food arrived shortly and after a while they were enjoying themselves with wonderful food and great conversation. Soon she had forgotten about the stares.

"For dessert we have key lime pie, cheesecake, and crème brulee." Eliza waited for their answer.

Colin looked at her. "I'm really stuffed."

"You're never too stuffed for dessert." Gabriela crossed her arms. "We'll have the cheesecake."

"Coffee with that?" Eliza seemed to have thawed towards her.

"Do you have English tea?" Gabriela arched her brow.

"We do."

"Two teas and we will share the cheesecake" Gabriela smiled.

"I'll have that right out." Eliza headed back to the kitchen.

"So have you had a good date?" Colin leaned back in his chair and studied her.

"Yes. This seems to have worked out for everyone. You get a date that's not psycho. And I get cheesecake."

He laughed out loud and more than a few people turned to stare.

Their cheesecake arrived and they ate in silence.

"I can't eat any more." Colin set his fork down and pushed the dessert toward Gabriela.

"Quitter." She finished off the dessert and then sat back and sighed.

Maxwell Higgins, the owner walked over and smiled at them both. "Was everything to your satisfaction?"

"It was wonderful." Colin nodded.

"Yes, the best meal I've had in a while." Gabriela agreed.

"Well that's high praise. You've spent some time in New York so I'm sure you've eaten at some of the finest restaurants." Maxwell looked pleased.

"None as good as your food." Gabriela complimented.

"I'd like to leave a tip." Colin pulled out his wallet.

"Oh please don't." Eliza appeared. "My service is part of the auction date."

Colin looked unsure.

"She's right." Maxwell assured.

Colin stood. "Thank you again."

"Any time. Enjoy the rest of your night." Maxwell headed over to the next table to speak to some customers.

They quietly left the restaurant and stepped out on the sidewalk. He walked around to the passenger's side of his car and opened the door for her.

As they drove back towards Aunt Agnes's house a part of Gabriela wished the date didn't have to end.

When he pulled up to the house, he started to get out.

"You don't have to walk me to the door."

"What kind of gentleman would I be if I just dropped you off?" He got out and hurried to her door.

She grinned and shook her head and stepped out of the car.

They walked to the front door. She noticed the porch light was on but everything inside the house was dark. Probably so Aunt Agnes could spy on them

"I had a really good time tonight." Her words were soft.

"I did too. I was going to try to squeeze in a round of golf but I was afraid you would beat me. I heard you're really good."

She threw her head back and laughed.

"Gabriela, I want to ask you something."

"Okay."

"I want to know if it would be okay if I kissed you."

"I've never had a guy ask me that before." She blinked.

"Well just so you know, I really want to. And I want to take you out again."

"You do?" Her heart thudded in her chest.

"Yes. I do."

"I think that would be okay."

"Okay to take you out? Or okay to kiss you?" His brows furrowed as he stared intently into her eyes.

She grinned. "Both are okay."

He leaned in and gently kissed her. When he pulled back they were both breathless.

"I should go inside." Gabriela felt her heart tumble in her chest.

"I'll call you tomorrow." Colin reached for her hand and kissed the back of her knuckles.

She felt her face heat as she stepped inside the house. She pressed her back against the door and closed her eyes.

Maybe things were looking up after all.

CHAPTER 28

Colin hardly slept. He'd spent the majority of night thinking of Gabriela.

Despite the lack of sleep he couldn't stop smiling as he walked toward the English Rose Bookstore. He didn't open the store on Sunday but he figured he would go in and get some writing done. When he got there Albert was waiting on him.

"Good morning Albert. How are you this morning." He pulled the keys out of his pocket and stuck them in the lock.

"Colin." He shifted his weight. "I'm guessing you've not seen the paper this morning."

"No. Just picked it up." He pulled it out from under his arm and wave it. "I figured I would enjoy reading it over a cup of tea." He stepped inside the bookstore and held the door open for Albert.

"Colin, I just wanted you to know that I was totally against running that story."

"What story?" Colin set his items down on the counter.

Albert ran his fingers through his hair. "The editor wanted to do a follow up of the successful auction and charity event. As he was looking up some background on Gabriela's time in new York he came across an article in one of those high society papers. It accused Gabriela of ruining a high profile photographer's career. It said that Gabriela didn't get the cover she wanted so she accused him of sexual harassment. Instead of getting him in trouble all it did was have her blackballed from any modeling agency wanting to work with her." Albert looked troubled.

"What?"

"Look, I can tell you really like her. But she has a history of well, ruining men."

Colin lifted his chin. "I prefer not to listen to idle gossip. I prefer to do my own research." He walked over to the door and held it open. "Now if you don't mind.."

Albert shook his head. "Again Colin, I'm sorry to be the one to tell you."

Instead of flipping the open sign in the door, he locked the door after Albert left. He had planned on getting some writing done but now he had another mission. A mission for the truth.

CHAPTER 29

"Gabriela, we need to talk about this." Aunt Agnes pounded on her door.

After getting up early and making coffee Gabriela had retrieved the newspaper from the mailbox. She had been shocked to see the story about her time in New York splattered on the front page.

"Go away." Crushed, she buried her face into the pillow. If she thought she had a chance of making a life in Harland Creek with Colin at her side, she knew now that would never happen. It was noon and he would have seen the newspaper by now. If not, she was sure half the town would have run to him to tell him about her past.

She couldn't stay here. Wiping her tears she climbed out of bed.

"Gabriela, open the door so we can talk."

"You're going to be late for church." She yelled as she got her suitcase out of the closet.

"There's not Sunday school today. I've got an hour before I have to be there. Plenty of time for us to talk."

Gabriela threw her clothes in the suitcase and the few minimal items she owned. She walked over and threw open the door. "I need to borrow the truck."

"For what?" Aunt Agnes frowned.

"Don't worry. I'll bring it back in time for you to be at church."

The older woman frowned but dug in her apron pocket and pulled out her keys.

She took the keys and grabbed her suitcase.

"Where are you going? Are you coming back?" Aunt Agnes looked concerned.

"Don't worry. By this afternoon, you won't have to worry about what your neighbors think anymore."

Aunt Agnes started to say something but Gabriela didn't bother waiting around to hear it. She was done with everyone and done with Harland creek.

She pulled out of the driveway and headed to town. She made it in record time.

She pulled into the almost empty church parking lot and killed the engine. The old truck backfired

The only car there belonged to Pastor John. Leaving her suitcase in the truck she walked up to the door and prayed it wouldn't be locked.

She tried the door and thankfully it wasn't locked. She stepped inside and called out. "Hello?"

Pastor John appeared from the back. "I'm here." When he spotted her he seemed surprised. "Gabriela. is everything okay?"

"No. It's not." She stepped toward him.

"What can I do to help you?" He truly looked concerned.

"Is forgiveness real? Like can someone really get forgiveness?" She looked at him.

"Please sit." He pointed to the pew.

She sat and he sat beside her. "Forgiveness starts with forgiving others." He looked over at her.

"What?" She jerked her head at him.

"I know. It's a hard thing. But with God everything is possible."

"Maybe for other people but not for me."

"Have you forgiven yourself?" He cocked his head.

"What?"

"Have you forgiven yourself for what happened in the past?"

"No. It's hard to forgive myself when other's keep holding it against me." She looked at her hands in her lap. "I'm just tired. I want to go somewhere that no one knows me and start over."

"What happened in the past was an accident, Gabriela. People had a hard time dealing with it because a young life was taken out of the world and when people don't see a reason behind it they want to blame someone."

"And now with that stupid newspaper article, it will just add fuel for the fire."

"So tell people the truth. Tell them exactly what happened."

"There's no point. They won't believe me. There's no hope for me. I'm leaving town."

"If you really believed there was no hope then you wouldn't be here. In church. Asking my advice." He gave her a gentle smile.

"I don't know." She stood.

He stood too. "Come back to the kitchen and have some coffee."

"Don't you have to get ready for church?" She could use some coffee but didn't want to impose on his time.

"I have plenty of time. No Sunday school today. Besides, I just got this fancy coffee in. Come have a cup."

She sighed.

"Fine. But only because I didn't get a chance to get any this morning."

"Great. I promise I won't keep you long.

CHAPTER 30

*C*olin didn't normally go to church. But since Albert had told him about the article he'd been doing some research on his own. And he sent up a prayer or two for Gabriela. He'd tried calling Agnes's house but no one answered. He figured the older woman would be at church and Gabriela would be laying low.

It was when he tracked down and called a model who'd worked with Gabriella that he stuck gold.

A knock on the door of his bookstore had him looking up from the computer.

"Colin. Open the door." Agnes beat on the door. She had Elizabeth with her.

He hurried over and let her in.

"Is Gabriela here?" She looked around the store.

"No, she took my truck this morning. And she took her suitcase with her. After she left I checked her room. She packed all her belongings." She wrung her hands. "After that story in the paper I just know she's leaving and not coming back."

"What?" His heart froze.

Elizabeth's cell phone rang and she answered it. She moved to the corner of the room to talk.

"Did she say where she was going?"

"No. And this time I don't think I'll ever see her again?" Agnes shook her head.

"I know where she is." Elizabeth hung up the phone. "That was Pastor John. He said Gabriela is at the church. He said he's trying to keep her there as long as he can but to hurry."

"I don't think she's going to want to see me." Agnes shook her head. "I didn't treat her so well when she won the auction date. I thought she would ruin you, Colin."

Colin shoved his hand through his hair. "Ms. Agnes. She didn't win the auction date. I begged to bid and win it.I even gave her the money to do it."

Agnes gave him a wide eyed stare. "But why?"

"Well at first because she got me involved in it. And I knew she wasn't interested in me. I knew she wouldn't' make me uncomfortable like the others who seemed so eager to go on a date. It was after spending time with her that I realized how very much I really liked her. I even asked her on another date. I know the townspeople haven't forgiven her for an accident wasn't even her fault. But I had hoped after really seeing who she was they would."

"Oh Colin. I had no idea." Agnes wiped her eyes. "But what about the article? In the newspaper?"

"That article should have been followed up to what really happened." He grabbed his laptop. "Come on. Let's get to the church before Gabriela leaves. We are going to put this to bed once and for all."

CHAPTER 31

*G*abriela glance at the time on her phone and nearly spit out her coffee. "Oh my gosh. You should have told me I was keeping you."

Pastor John stood quickly. "Oh you're not keeping me. We hardly ever start on time. Would you like another cup of coffee?"

"No, I really have to get going."

"Gabriela, I really think you should stay. After all you told me about what happened in New York, I think you should stay and tell your side of the story." He gave her arm a gentle squeeze.

"It wouldn't matter." She put her coffee cup in the sink and grabbed her purse "Would you do me a favor?"

"Of course."

"Can you call Aunt Agnes and tell her I'm leaving her truck at the bus station." She glanced at the time. "I have to hurry over there if I'm going to leave today."

"Okay. If that's what you really want."

"And thanks for listening. And not judging." She nodded.

"Any time." Pastor John smiled.

She headed into the sanctuary. If she hurried she could make it out of the church parking lot before anyone saw her.

She hiked her purse on her shoulder hurried to the sanctuary.

The second she stepped inside she froze. People were already sitting quietly in pews. Standing in the aisle was Colin and her aunt who was still dressed in her overalls and weird hat.

"Excuse me." She ducked her head and tried to walk around them but Colin grabbed her arm

"Wait. There's something I need to say."

"Colin, I know you saw the article and I don't…"

"No." He lifted his chin. "I have something to say and I'm going to say it. In front of everyone."

She felt a little faint. The last thing she wanted was to be yelled at in front of the whole town by Colin.

"I saw the paper."

She ducked her head and braced herself.

"And I did a little research myself." He grabbed his computer from the pew. "That article was put out months ago. I tracked down a follow up to that article and what I found was…" He turned and faced the audience "I found that Gabriela didn't get the cover because she refused the advances of that photographer. After she came forward other models started coming forward. She didn't ruin his career. He did that to himself. I even have an email from a model I contacted who backs up Gabriela's story. In fact, Gabriela probably saved other girls from this predatory photographer."

The congregation gave each other looks of astonishment.

Missy stood up. "She is still responsible for the death of Ricky."

Nausea rolled through her stomach. She wanted to leave but Colin tightened his grip on her arm and shook his head.

Travis stood up from the back pew. His face was ashen. "No she's not. I'm the reason Ricky is dead."

A collective gasp rose through the people and Gabriela looked on in astonishment.

"Travis, is there somewhere you would like to talk privately?" Pastor John stepped forward.

"No. There is something the town doesn't know and I've kept this secret for years. And it's eating me up inside. I was there the night of the accident. Gabriela tried to tell the police that but they didn't believe her. And when they got around to asking me I lied. I was a kid and I was scared so I lied." Tears rolled down his face.

Gabriela's mouth dropped open. She looked at Colin. He looked as stunned as she felt.

"I encouraged Ricky to make that jump. I mean, I'd done it a ton of times. I didn't realize the water was that low. When he asked me if he'd be safe I said yeah. He was trying to impress her but I'm the one who told him it was safe." He buried his face in his hands and wept.

No one moved. They were too stunned.

No one moved but her.

Slowly she walked toward Travis. When she reached him, he looked up at her. "You must hate me. You'll never hate me as much as I hate myself."

She shook her head. "I don't hate you. It was an accident. Thank you for telling everyone the truth. Even if it is late."

He looked at her stunned. "How can you forgive me?"

"Because this has gone on too long. I don't have the energy to hold a grudge. And because I am forgiven, I am compelled to forgive."

When he went into her arms, she held him while he cried.

Sloan stood up and came up to them. Travis looked up and held his arms about. "I guess you are arresting me."

"No son. But I do need to get you to make a statement at

the police station. So it will be on record. You can call your parents to meet you there."

Travis nodded. He looked back at her. "Thank you Gabriela."

She nodded feeling the weight of the world lift off her shoulders.

For the first time in a while she felt like she could fly.

"Gabriela, I owe you an apology." Aunt Agnes touched her arm.

Gabriela turned.

"I have treated you unfairly and I'm sorry. I'm so very sorry. Will you forgive an old woman?" A tear ran down her face.

"I do." She smiled.

Aunt Agnes pulled her into a tight hug. When they finally pulled apart, Gabriela realized the whole congregation had lined up to ask for her forgiveness.

By the time it was over, there was not a dry eye in the church.

CHAPTER 32

"*I* don't know why you just don't stay at my house."
Aunt Agnes scowled as she swept the room.

"Because I know how you like your space. Besides having my own place will be good for both of us." Gabriela finished making up the bed in the bedroom. "Besides if I didn't snap up Olivia's house to rent someone else would."

"I can't believe she and Sam ran off and got married. I would have put money on Heather and Grayson getting married first." Agnes shook her head.

"Olivia said after watching her friend Alexandria get married and how big of a mess that turned into she wanted something simple. A wedding in a chapel in Gatlinburg. Besides, they are planning on spending all their money on an elaborate honeymoon. I think it's smart."

"That's true." Her aunt agreed. "But I don't believe you'll have much time for me anymore. Not will all this freelance work you have."

"I'll still have time to help with your subscription boxes." Gabriela laughed.

"I can' believe I was missing out on so much money. Since

you started keeping my books, I seem to have money I didn't know about. Not to mention how many subscription boxes I've sold. I can't believe how many orders I've gotten." She shook her head.

"Honey and honey products are a hot commodity. People love homemade items." She shrugged and looked at her calendar. "I've got to finish a marketing plan for Colin's new book. And then I've been hired to come up with an e-commerce store for Stacey to help sell her clothes."

"Not to mention all the other offers you keep getting from out of state.' Her aunt shook her head. "I don't know how you keep it straight.

"Well, I like to stay busy." She stood and looked at the bedroom. "Thanks for helping me get moved in. I'm lucky Olivia is renting the house fully furnished. That way I can save my money and hopefully make an offer to buy it in the near future."

"I wouldn't plan that far ahead. By the way you and Colin have been courting, I fully expect you guys to get married next."

"Whoa whoa. I'm not ready to hear those words yet." She arched her brow.

Someone knocked on the front door. She turned and headed to answer it.

She opened the door without looking who it was and Ringo waltzed right in with Colin behind him. She bent and gave the dog some kisses on his head.

"What about me?" Colin stood with his hands spread out.

She laughed and stood. "I was getting to you." She kissed him.

"I brought over something you could use." He held out a bag.

She frowned and reached inside. She pulled out a laptop computer.

"Colin, I can't believe you got me this."

"I know it's hard working when you're having to split your time between the bookstore and library to use their computer. I thought it would come in handy."

"Thank you." She threw herself in his arm and hugged him tight

"What's this now?" Aunt Agnes appeared and grinned.

"Look what Colin bought me." She held up the computer.

"Oh wow. And here I thought a way to a woman's heart was flowers and jewelry. But no, it's with a computer."

They laughed.

"And I also have this." He held out a white box.

She took it and carefully opened it. Inside was a copy of his book.

"Oh Colin, it's beautiful. And I have so many ideas of how to market this."

"Read the acknowledgements." He nodded.

She carefully turned to the page.

This book is dedicated to Gabriela Jackson. She taught me how to forgive and to live each moment to its fullest. But most importantly she taught me how to love.

She will forever hold my heart.

"Oh Colin." She threw her arms around his neck.

"In case you don't know and need to hear it, I love you deeply." He whispered against her hair.

Tears burned the backs of her eyes. "I love you too. And I can't wait to see where it takes us."

THE END

ABOUT THE AUTHOR

Jodi Allen Brice has written numerous books under a different pen name. Under Jodi Allen Brice she writes fiction and small town clean and sweet romance.

She transitioned away from paranormal romance in the year 2020 when the virus hit. She said she felt she needed to write a book that would change hearts and minds where Christ is concerned. She is a Christian who loves studying Bible prophesy and spending time with her family in Arkansas. She's is also an avid quilter and camping. Sometimes she does both at the same time!

Her favorite Bible verse is I Corinthians 15:51-52

"In a flash, in the twinkling of an eye, at the last trumpet. For the trumpet will sound, the dead will be raised imperishable, and we will be changed."

John 3:16 "For God so loved the world that he gave his one and only son, so whosoever believes in Him shall not perish but have eternal life."

Check out her website at http://jodiallenbrice.com

ALSO BY JODI ALLEN BRICE

Novels

So This Is Goodbye

Not Like the Other Girls

Harland Creek Series

Promise Kept

Promise Made

Promise Forever

Harland Creek Quilter's Mystery Series

Mystery of the Drunkards Path

Check out http://jodiallenbrice.com for all the latest releases!

Novels

So This Is Goodbye

Not Like the Other Girls

Harland Creek Series

Promise Kept

Promise Made

Promise Forever

Harland Creek Quilter's Mystery Series

Mystery of the Drunkards Path